D1254032

SAINT JOHN BOSCO
AND THE CHILDREN'S SAINT,
DOMINIC SAVIO

SAINT JOHN BOSCO
AND THE CHILDREN'S SAINT
DOMINIC SAVIO

Written by Catherine Beebe

Illustrated by Robb Beebe

IGNATIUS PRESS   SAN FRANCISCO

Original edition © 1955 by Robb Beebe
Originally published by Farrar, Straus & Cudahy, Inc.
A Vision Book
Published with ecclesiastical approval
Reprinted with permission of
Farrar, Straus & Giroux, Inc.

Cover design by Riz Boncan Marsella
Cover illustration by Christopher J. Pelicano

Published by Ignatius Press, San Francisco, 1992
All rights reserved
ISBN 978-0-89870-416-7
Library of Congress catalogue number 92-71930
Printed in the United States of America

For all our children

CHAPTER ONE

"HE CAN PICK COINS right out of your ears!" shouted an excited eleven-year-old boy.

"And he can toss three good-sized soup bowls, one after the other, high in the air, and keep them there without dropping them!" his friend cried breathlessly.

"I saw him walk a tightrope tied from one tree to another", yelled a third boy with awe in his voice. "He walked the whole way, as far as from here to there." He pointed to a spot ten feet away from where the group was standing. "And without once falling off!"

"I don't believe a word of it", sneered the boy to whom they were telling these tales. "I'd have to see these tricks with my own eyes, my very own eyes, before I'd believe you."

"Well, come along and see for yourself", said the other three boys.

Off they ran, all four of them, down the winding street to the village square.

"Where is he?" asked the doubting Thomas. "Where is your friend with his magic tricks? I don't see him."

"He isn't here." The three boys showed their surprise and disappointment. "He must have gone away for some reason. Let's come back tomorrow. He'll be here then. He said that he would."

"And you believed him?" scoffed the other young fellow.

"Sure we did!" his three friends declared. "He's not the kind to lie."

"How do you know that?" the other fellow wanted to know. These boys weren't going to fool him! Not if he could help it!

"Well, I know he didn't lie", said the first boy. "There was something about him. I can't say just what it was, but it made me feel deep down inside that he wouldn't lie to us."

"No, nor to anyone else!" The other two had seen the juggler and magician, and they agreed with the first boy.

"He was funny and full of fun, but I'm sure he

wouldn't say anything that wasn't true", the first boy stated positively.

They were quite right, for the juggler and magician they had seen in the village square was John Bosco. At that time he was no better known than any other boy in his Italian village. But that same John Bosco was to become known and loved all over the world. He was to be remembered, not for his tricks of magic or for his skill as a tightrope walker, but as one of the world's mighty saints.

He was born on the sixteenth of August in the year 1815 in a village outside Turin, Italy. A few days later the baby was baptized and given the name John Melchior. One of the three wise men who brought gifts to the infant Jesus was named Melchior. But the baby never used that name. He was known from the beginning as John Bosco.

John's father, Francis Bosco, was a farmer. His small house was built on the side of a hill in a little place called Becchi. There was only a little land around the cottage, and it was not good land for farming. Francis Bosco had to work very hard to raise enough food for his family, but he didn't have the money to buy a better farm. He and his wife did the best they could with what they had.

Francis Bosco worked very hard from early morning until late at night. He plowed the ground, planted the seed, and harvested the crops as each season came. He was a strong man but the heavy farm work and the long hours in all kinds of weather were more than even the strongest man could bear. He became ill and within a few days died of pneumonia.

His youngest child John was only two years old when this great sorrow came to the family. His brother Joseph cried bitterly. He couldn't understand why their father was no longer with them. When their mother told John that his father would never return, he understood. Even at the age of two, John Bosco knew what it meant to be without a father.

Anthony, their half-brother, knew something of the meaning of death, for his mother had died when he was just a little boy. Anthony and his father lived alone for a long time, but finally the young widower could no longer bear his loneliness. It was then that he met Margaret Occhiena and married her. They were very happy together.

Margaret was a good and loving wife to Francis Bosco and a devoted mother to his son. Later they had two boys of their own. Their years together were happy ones until death brought its sorrow.

Margaret Bosco now had to be both mother and father to the three boys. She had her own work to do in taking care of them, and she also had to earn money to support them. There could be little time for tears. When she told her boys how hard it would be, they put their arms around her and said, "We'll help you, mother." And they did.

The two older boys helped with the farm work,

but young John's help was in the comfort that he gave his mother. He was a lovable little fellow who was always smiling. He was quite thoughtful and eager to please.

By the time John was four, he too had learned quite a bit about farm work. His brothers had taught him to gather firewood for cooking. He learned to draw water from the well and carry it to the kitchen for his mother. He picked and cleaned the vegetables that grew in the garden, and he ran many helpful errands.

The little boy got up very early each morning. He was ready and waiting when Anthony started for the pasture.

"Why do you always want to tag along?" Anthony asked with a frown.

"I like to go with you when you take the cattle to the meadow", John answered, taking two steps for each of his big brother's long ones.

"Why don't you just stay at home? You could play around and have some fun. It's silly for you to walk all that way every day." Anthony was annoyed. He was a big fellow of seven. He didn't want his little brother forever following him.

"Please let me go with you", John begged. "I like to watch the clouds above the meadow. God is very near to me there."

"Well, you are indeed a silly. Don't you know that God is everywhere?" asked Anthony.

"Yes, I do know that," John answered, "but I

can think about him much better when I can look up and see heaven right over my head."

Margaret Bosco had taught her boys well about God and his nearness to them. But it was to John, her youngest, that her teaching meant the most.

She had not been sent to school when she was growing up. In those days parents had to pay for their children's schooling and books. Margaret's father and mother did not have enough money for those things. Then too they needed her help to care for her many brothers and sisters. But Margaret's mother and the parish priest were careful to teach her the truths of her religion.

When she married Francis Bosco, she was able to teach her children all that she had learned. She was able to pass on to them her own deep love for the truths and beauty of their religion.

Her youngest son John was a deeply religious boy, but also a normal, healthy one. He was always full of energy and fun and sometimes full of mischief. He was big and strong, and he had a good mind.

Often when his mother sent him on errands to the nearby village, John stopped to play with other boys. Many a time he came home with a black eye or a lump on his head. One day he returned home with both.

"Now what were you up to?" his mother exclaimed when he came into the kitchen. "How many times have I told you to stay away from those rough fellows? Here you are with a bruised face and torn clothes. You must have been fighting again."

By this time John had poured water into a bowl and was trying to wash away the stains of battle. His mother left her cooking to help him.

"Why do you disobey me, John?" she asked. "I've told you not to have anything to do with those boys. They're bad ones."

"They're not really bad, Mother", John insisted. "They don't have the good mother I have to teach them right from wrong."

By this time his eye didn't hurt quite so much, and he was putting on a clean shirt.

His mother went back to her bread-making, and John could see a smile on her lips. He was pleased that she was no longer cross with him. He went to her and kissed her on her cheek.

"Please forgive me, Mother", he begged. "It's not that I mean to disobey, but I do have a good reason for playing with those boys."

"It must be a good one, John, for you know that disobedience is a venial sin. Let me hear it." She patted the last loaf into shape ready for baking and brushed the flour from her hands.

John helped her carry the loaves to the hearth. "You do so much for us, Mother", he said. "I wish that I could always please you."

"You usually do", she replied with a smile. Her anger was gone. "But I can't let a child of mine disobey. That would be my sin. Tell me quickly now. Why do you feel that you must play with those rough boys?"

For a moment John didn't answer. Then he said, "Their language is bad, mother, very bad. They say wicked things, and they swear. Oh, it's really frightening!"

"There, you see!" exclaimed his mother. "That is one of the reasons why I want you to stay away from them."

"But when I'm with them they don't say such things. And if they do, I can stop them." He flexed the muscles of his strong right arm.

"That doesn't seem to me the best way to teach goodness", his mother said with a frown. Then she softened a bit. "Perhaps you can do them some good. But guard yourself, my son. It is more likely that bad companions will pull you down than that you will raise them up."

She left him to think about her words while she washed and put away her mixing bowl. Then she sat down before the fire and began to mend the torn blouse.

"How I wish your father were still here", she sighed. "He'd know so much better than I how to teach his sons."

After his most recent battle with the village boys John's mother kept him at home. She sent his brothers to run her errands in the village. She found work for John to do around the house and farm.

One day on his way to the pasture with the cows,

he discovered that a nightingale had built a nest in a tree close to his path. He started looking into the nest every morning. He was very gentle and quiet about it, and the little bird soon learned that he was her friend. He brought her crumbs which she ate from his fingers without showing any fear.

One day John found that the eggs had opened and the baby birds were hatched.

"They're such funny looking things", he told his mother. "They look as if they were all mouths."

"That's because they are always hungry. You'll need more crumbs for your bird family." She gave him bread from her own breakfast for the baby nightingales.

"I suppose someday they'll turn into beautiful birds and fly away", John said. "But right now it's hard to picture that."

His little birds were never to become beautiful and fly away. One day on his way to the pasture John saw a terrible sight. When he was still far away from the tree he heard the frightened cry of the mother bird. Before he could reach the nest, a large cuckoo had swooped down. She killed all the little birds as well as the mother who tried so bravely to save them.

"Oh, you cruel bird!" John shouted. "I'd like to wring your neck!" He shook his fist at the cuckoo who was sitting high up in the branches.

The empty nest was still there but the whole family had been killed.

John felt very sad that day. While he took care

of the sheep and the cows on the hillside pasture, he couldn't think of anything but the nightingale family. On his way home he stopped at the tree. To his great surprise, he saw the cuckoo sitting in the nightingale's nest on an egg of her own.

"You're not only cruel," John shouted angrily, "but you are a killer and a robber also."

He ran home as fast as he could. He stumbled as he went, for tears blinded his eyes.

He didn't return to the pasture the next day. Joseph offered to watch the sheep for him. He understood how much the nightingale family meant to his brother and was sorry for him.

When John felt able to pass his special tree again, he didn't feed the cuckoo. He didn't like her well enough for that.

One day when he was still quite far from the tree, he saw a cat slinking along in the tall grass. Before John could reach him, he had climbed the tree and was down again, licking his chops over the cuckoo he had so swiftly eaten.

John's bird adventure was still not ended. Before a day had passed, another nightingale came to live in the nest. John looked in and saw to his amazement that she was sitting on the cuckoo's egg!

"You don't know what kind of a child you're hatching", John warned the nightingale. But she paid no attention to him.

Finally the baby cuckoo was hatched. The mother nightingale fed it as though it were her own. John brought the bird crumbs each day, and she, like the other nightingale, became his friend.

One day he discovered that the mother bird was gone. The baby was alone and hungry.

"You poor little thing", John said. He looked around for the nightingale but couldn't find her. "Maybe the old cat got her too", he said. "I'd better take you home where you'll be safe."

As he came near the house he called out, "Joseph, Anthony, I have a baby cuckoo. Come and help me build a cage for it."

The two boys came running. "Why do you want to build a cage for that old bird?" Anthony asked in great disgust. "He'll only grow up to be a killer."

John had thought of that too. But he also thought, "Maybe if I take good care of him and keep him warm and well fed, he might turn out to be a good bird. He might even turn out to be like the nightingale."

But John's pet didn't live long enough for him to find out. One morning he found the bird dead. It lay stiff and cold on the floor of the cage.

"I wouldn't be too sorry about that", Anthony said. "After all you can't make a nightingale out of a cuckoo."

But his youngest brother thought otherwise.

CHAPTER TWO

O NE MORNING AT BREAKFAST John sat playing
with his food. He didn't eat with his usual
hearty enjoyment. His brothers didn't notice anything unusual, but his mother did.

"Are you ill, Johnny?" she asked. "You haven't
taken even one swallow of your milk."

He didn't hear her for his thoughts were far away.

She rose from the table and went to him. She
put her hand to his forehead. "You have no fever,
John", she said. "Is something troubling you?"

He smiled and began to eat. "I'm all right, mother", he said. "It's just that I had the strangest dream last night. I can't get it out of my mind."

"Sometimes I have dreams too", Joseph said.

"And so do I", Anthony added. "Some are pretty good ones, and some are nightmares. But they don't keep me from eating."

"Dreams don't usually bother me either", John explained. "But this one was different."

"Maybe if you told us about it you might be able to forget it", his mother said.

"But, Mother, I don't want to forget it. I really believe that I must remember this one all my life." The boy's eyes sparkled as if he had just thought of something exciting.

"Now you're more like yourself", said Joseph, smiling at his little brother.

"All this fuss over a dream! It's just silly", Anthony said crossly.

"Don't say that, Tony." His mother silenced him with a look. "I don't think John's dream was silly. Let him tell us about it."

"I'll try", said John. "It was all so real. I can still see the people in it. I was in a big field, perhaps it was a meadow like our own. Anyway there were many boys there. They were yelling and screaming and playing very rough games. They were even worse than the boys in the village. They cursed and swore and said things that I was ashamed to

19

hear. I became very angry and rushed in and began to pound them. I fought hard.

"Suddenly I heard a voice say, 'Be gentle with them. You'll not win their friendship that way—not with blows but with kindness.'

"I turned around and saw a man who was very beautiful."

"Men aren't beautiful", Anthony scoffed.

"This one was", John replied positively.

"Never mind that", said their mother. "Go on with your dream."

" 'Be gentle with them' ", John repeated. " 'You'll not win their friendship that way—not with blows but with kindness.'

"While I watched, those rough boys turned into wild beasts. They charged around, knocking each other down and bumping into each other. It was a terrible sight. I didn't want to look at it, but I had to.

"Then before I knew what had happened, they had all become little woolly lambs. They began to play peacefully and happily together in the big meadow.

"The beautiful man spoke again. 'Teach them right from wrong', he said. 'Teach them the beauty of goodness and the ugliness of sin.'

" 'How can I do that?' I asked. 'I don't know how to teach. I've never been to school. I don't know anything.' "

"You were certainly right there", said Anthony. "You really don't know anything."

"Stop that, Anthony", his mother scolded him. "Go on, John."

Her youngest son smiled at her. It was good to have a mother who understood. John went on with the story of his dream. "I began to cry because I couldn't do what the beautiful man asked. I wanted so much to please him. He comforted me, and I stopped crying.

" 'Try to do as I have told you', he said. 'If you make the effort and keep trying, I will help you. First I will give you the best of all teachers. She was my first teacher. She will show you how to do all things with love, patience, and strength.' He looked over my head and smiled in a way I shall never forget. I turned to see who he was smiling at and I saw.

"Oh, mother, you can't imagine how beautiful she was. Beautiful isn't the right word. She was so much more than that. I just can't tell you what she was like. I don't know any words to describe her.

" 'I shall teach you', she said. 'Someday you will understand.'

"Then they were both gone, the lovely lady and the beautiful man."

John was silent. He would never forget them nor his strange and wonderful dream.

"Perhaps your dream means that you are going to be a shepherd and have the biggest flock of sheep in all Italy", Joseph said.

"More likely it means that you are going to lead a band of pirates or robbers", Anthony said.

"It's not right to put meanings into dreams," their mother warned, "nor to believe in them."

"But this wasn't an ordinary dream", John insisted.

"No, it wasn't", his mother agreed. "Maybe your strange dream means that you are to be a priest. Maybe you will take care of one of the Good Shepherd's flocks. Ask God to show you what he wants you to do when you grow up. Ask his Blessed Mother to make you strong enough to do it. Now be off with you, boys. There's work waiting to be done."

The boys went their separate ways, and Margaret was alone with her thoughts and her dreams. She must pray more now than she had ever prayed before. Perhaps her Johnny was meant to be a priest. But how would she pay for his schooling? Well, if the good Lord wanted John to be a priest, he'd show her how to help her son.

"If only I could be a priest", thought John as he milked the cow. "If only I could be a priest", he thought as he swept the stable. "If only I could be a priest", he thought as he chopped the firewood. "If only I could be a priest", he thought as he snuggled down into his bed at night.

The thought never left him. He didn't talk about his great longing, but it was always there in his mind and heart.

One day when John and his mother were returning from the village market, they passed an old priest.

"Good afternoon, Father", John said eagerly. It seemed so wonderful to talk to a priest.

"Good afternoon, my son", the priest smiled at him and nodded to his mother. Then he walked on down the road.

John walked along in silence for quite a while.

"Why are you so quiet, Johnny?" his mother asked. "What are you thinking about?"

"I'm thinking about the priest who just passed by. I wish he'd stopped and talked with us." His voice showed how disappointed he was.

"Priests are busy people, Johnny", his mother explained. "They don't have time to talk with everyone they meet."

"If I were a priest, I'd have time", John declared. "I'd always have time to talk with boys. Oh, Mother, if I could be a priest that's what I'd do. I'd take care of boys. I'd be a real father to them. I'd talk to them, and they could talk to me whenever they wanted to. I'd never be too busy for that. Boys would be my special work. I do wish that I could be a priest."

"Oh, Johnny, Johnny, if only you could", his mother sighed.

"Would you really want me to be?" he asked in surprise. He had often wondered what his mother would say if she knew his thoughts about it.

"Yes, dear, I'd be so very happy. But I'm afraid that it isn't possible for boys like you. Priests must go to school for many years. They must know a great deal, because they have to teach their people as well as pray for them. How could you get all the schooling that is needed for such great work? You've had no schooling at all, and I have no way of earning the money to pay for even the simplest lessons."

"There must be a way, Mother", John said positively. "I know that God wants me to be a priest. I've been sure of that ever since my dream."

"Well, if our Lord is calling you to serve him, he will show you the way", his mother replied. "We must pray about it, Johnny."

And pray they did, with great fervor and strong faith. Margaret could see no way for her son to get the education he would need to become a priest. But if the time ever came when he could go to school, there would be one subject he would know very well. That subject was his religion. She had been able to teach him that.

Although Margaret Bosco could not read or write, she had learned her prayers and catechism and Bible stories from her own mother and their parish priest. When she was a young girl she had learned many verses from the Bible by heart and could say them from memory. As her boys grew up she was able to pass on to them these treasures of knowledge and faith.

Her teaching didn't mean a great deal to Joseph and Anthony. They listened and learned and hurried away as soon as they could.

This was not true of John. He loved every story his mother told and always begged for more. Often he sat with her on the doorstep watching the stars come out one by one.

"They look like candles being lighted", he would say.

"They are God's candles", was his mother's quiet answer. "They're being lighted by God's unseen hand. They have come out to praise him. 'All the works of the Lord . . . praise and glorify him forever.' Do you remember those verses, Johnny?"

"Oh, yes, Mother," he replied at once, "and the one that goes, 'Praise him, sun and moon; praise him, all you twinkling stars.' I like that one the best."

Margaret Bosco told her children all the Bible stories she had learned. John never tired of hearing them, and he never forgot what she said.

About this time, John Bosco started learning the tricks of the acrobats and jugglers who gave shows at Castlenuova, three miles away. Twice a week he went to market there with his mother to sell their farm products. While she bargained with the stall owners and bought the few things needed at home, John wandered off to see what was going on.

Each market day traveling players gave a show on the village green. The boys and girls of the town as well as those who came to market went to see it.

John loved to watch these shows. He'd find a place right down in front. The actors were usually skilled jugglers, acrobats, or magicians. They were so quick with their tricks that no one could see how they did them.

Quick as they were, John's eyes and mind were quicker. He watched them carefully and remembered all that he saw: Back home he practiced what he had seen over and over again. Before long he could do the tricks as well as the traveling players.

Joseph enjoyed watching his brother do tricks. He admired John's skill, but he did not have any desire to learn the tricks himself.

Anthony thought the whole thing was silly and a great waste of time.

"It's not a waste of time", John declared, trying not to be angry.

"Are you planning to be a wandering juggler?" his oldest brother scoffed.

"No, I'm not", John answered. "But I'm going to use these tricks for a very good purpose."

"A good purpose!" Anthony laughed loudly. "For what purpose, good or bad, could you possibly use tumbling or tossing bowls into the air? What purpose can there be in turning sticks into flowers? What purpose is there in pulling rabbits that you can't eat out of a hat? Brother John, you must be crazy!"

"I'm not crazy", John protested. "And let me tell you I'm going to use everything that I've learned or ever will learn for a very good purpose—in fact, for the best purpose in the world."

He wasn't telling anyone what that purpose was, but in his own heart he knew. With the help of God and the Blessed Mother, John Bosco knew he could fulfill that purpose.

Whenever John could be spared from his work, he hurried to the village. His mother no longer worried about his playing with the rough boys as long as they weren't truly evil. John seldom came home now with a black eye or torn clothes. He had found a better way than fighting to win them for friends.

As soon as he reached the village he would look around for a group of young people. When he found them playing together or just talking, he would say, "Want to see me take a penny out of your ear?"

Before there was time to answer, John had done just that. "How about you?" he'd say to another boy.

"There's no penny in my ear", the boy would reply. "It would be safe in my pocket or else buying me something good to eat."

While he was still talking, John would hold up a penny that he had taken out of the ear of the astonished boy.

Then the whole crowd would begin shouting, "Take one out of my ear."

"And mine."

"No, mine next."

In no time at all a great crowd of pushing, shouting boys and girls gathered around him. Then John would elbow his way out of the crowd and climb upon the lowest branches of a tree.

"Step this way", he'd call out. "Step this way to see the greatest show in Castlenuova. Tumbling, juggling, magic, even tightrope walking—I can do them all."

At first the crowd did not believe that statement. He'd have to prove it. They'd have to see for themselves.

"Show us your tricks, John Bosco", they'd shout. "Be quick about it too." There was a threat in their voices and their manner.

"Patience, patience!" John would smile at them. "We must have quiet before the show begins."

As soon as the crowd became quiet, he called out, "People who come to shows have to pay to see them."

A great roar went up from the crowd.

"I knew there was some fake about it", said one young fellow as he turned to walk away. His friends started to follow him.

"Come back! All of you, come back", John cried out. "You don't need money to pay for this show. The pay is something any one of you can give easily. Just say a decade of the Rosary with me. Then I'll do my best tricks for you."

The crowd was silent. A prayer to pay for a show! It had been a long time since most of them had said a prayer. They used God's name only in swearing.

John waited, not saying a word but praying that they would accept his price.

Finally one boy broke the silence. "A few prayers are not too much to pay", he shouted. "But the show had better be good."

He was the leader of the gang. Whatever he did the others followed. Usually he led them into mischief or wrongdoing. But he was their leader. If he was willing to say a prayer for the show, they'd do it too.

"I'm willing", yelled one of his followers.

The others took up the cry.

Once more John asked for silence. Then he began, "In the name of the Father and of the Son and of the Holy Spirit, amen. Our Father who art in heaven . . ." His young voice rang out clearly.

He said the prayer slowly, and the children joined in.

As soon as the prayer was ended, John began doing his tricks and stunts. His long hours of practice had made him quite skillful. The bumps and bruises from his first tries at tumbling had all been worthwhile. He did each stunt perfectly.

John Bosco had taken his first step toward his strong purpose. He had attracted a group of unruly young people toward our Lady with her own special prayer.

One market day while John was doing tricks for the young people, his mother went to see the pastor of the church near the market. She was worrying about John, and she had decided to talk with the priest about him.

"My son knows his catechism very well, Father, and he has a deep love of God and the Blessed Mother. He needs the graces and help that only the sacraments can give him. May he receive his first Holy Communion?"

"But, Mrs. Bosco, your boy is only ten years old", said the priest. "That is too young. Our children are not allowed to receive holy Eucharist until they are twelve or older."

"Yes, I know, Father," she replied, "but he is not like other boys. If only you'd talk to him, I'm sure you'd see for yourself. May he come to you, Father? Will you talk to him?"

The priest smiled. Each mother thought her own child was different. "Yes, send the boy to me tomorrow. If he is ready to receive our Lord, I'll give my permission."

"Thank you, Father. Thank you." Margaret hurried away to find John.

As they walked home she told him about her visit.

"Oh, Mother, if only I can receive our Lord, I'll be the happiest boy in the world." He hopped on one foot and then on the other. He was too excited to walk quietly.

"Don't get your hopes too high, John", she said. "Remember you are only ten years old. You may have to wait two more years."

The next day, in his best clothes and with his hair slicked down smoothly, John went alone to Castlenuova. When he reached the town, he went directly to the church for a visit. Then he walked to the rectory and rang the bell.

The pastor came to the door. "Come in, my boy. I'm glad to see you." He led the way to his study.

When the priest had finished questioning John, he said, "You have been taught well, my boy. What book have you been using?"

"I didn't have a book, Father", John replied. "I don't read very well. My mother taught me all I know about my religion."

"Didn't your mother use a book?" The priest felt sure that some book must have been used. The boy had answered all his questions unusually well.

"My mother doesn't know how to read either, but she knows all about our religion, Father", John answered proudly.

"Remarkable!" The priest sat back in his chair

and looked thoughtfully at the boy. "If you did that well without knowing how to read, think how much better you would do if you knew how. Would you like to learn to read?"

"I'd like to very much", the boy replied eagerly.

"We shall see." The priest stood up, and John knew that it was time for him to leave. "Tell that good mother of yours that she has done well. You may come back tomorrow and join our First Communion class. You are ready now. God bless you, my son." He made the sign of the cross over a very happy boy.

John went to the First Communion class until the great day finally came. That morning he was awake long before the roosters crowed. Usually they were his alarm clock, but he had no need for anyone to awaken him that day.

Early as it was, his mother was up before him. She had laid out clean clothes for him, and she herself was dressed in her Sunday best.

"Oh, Mother, you are beautiful!" John exclaimed.

She smiled at him. "No, Johnny, I'm really very plain, but inside I do feel beautiful. This is such a happy day for you and for me. When you welcome our Lord into your heart, remember your father, dear. How I wish he were with us to share our joy."

"He is with us, Mother, I'm sure. He will be

watching us from heaven." He gave his hair a final pat. "I'm ready now. Let's hurry. I don't want to be late."

Neither John nor his mother talked very much on the way to church. Each had thoughts that couldn't easily be put into words.

It was Easter Sunday, and both of them thought they had never seen a more beautiful day. They reached the church early and went inside to kneel at the altar rail. Then John took his place with the other children who were going to receive their First Communion, and his mother found her place with the parents.

Mass began. When the time came for holy Communion, Margaret watched her son walk quietly to the altar rail and kneel with the others.

"If I am to serve you as a priest, dear Lord," John prayed, "please show me the way."

His mother's prayer was for the same intention.

They were both quiet on the way home. The beauty of the holy occasion needed no words. It was only when they were almost home, that Margaret spoke.

"We'll now be doing the everyday things again, Johnny. But we shall do them better because of this holy day. I pray that God will stay in your heart, my son. Promise him to keep it good and pure as long as you live. Receive him often in Holy Communion. Be honest in your confessions. Be obedient always. Study your catechism and listen to the words of the priest. Keep away from bad companions."

Those were really the words of his mother on John Bosco's First Communion day. Years later when he was an old man, he still remembered them.

He wrote them in a book, and under her words, he added, "I tried to carry out her advice, and from that day on, my life seemed to be improving. Above all, I learned to obey and submit, although before then I often used to set my own wishes against any orders given by those over me."

As the weeks went by, John did the same things that he had done before his First Holy Communion. But now, as his mother had said, he did them better. His purpose in life became clearer and clearer to him. His longing to help other boys became stronger. He felt sorry for those who did not have a good home and a wonderful mother like his mother.

"If those boys had someone to love and teach them as I've been taught," he would say to his mother, "I'm sure they'd become good and useful. If they only knew how much God loves them, they wouldn't want to hurt him by their sins. If I could be a priest, I'd give my whole life to teaching boys."

He began to pray harder that God would show him the way to become a priest.

John kept on giving his shows. Often he made the crowd listen to a story as well as say some prayers before he would do any tricks for them. The stories were always from the Bible or some sermon he had heard. No one seemed to mind paying this unusual price to see his shows. In fact, they enjoyed the stories almost as much as the tricks.

A few of the rougher boys would turn away. They wouldn't listen to such holy nonsense. They changed their minds when they found they really couldn't see the show without paying the price. John's shows were worth watching.

CHAPTER THREE

Not long after his First Communion something happened which seemed a direct answer to John's prayer. A mission was being given in another village three miles away. Most of the people who lived near the Bosco family walked there and back twice each day to attend the services. Among the group was a priest whom John had never seen before.

He was an old man and very kind. He enjoyed the walk with the villagers. They all joined in friendly talks as they went to and from the church.

One evening the priest noticed John. He was listening with great interest to the talk about the fine mission sermons.

"Which sermon did you like best?" the priest asked John.

"I liked them all, Father", was the quick reply.

"But did you understand any of them?" asked the priest.

"Yes, Father", said John. "I understood all of them."

Some of the people laughed. The sermons had been given by a famous preacher. They were not the kind that a young boy could easily understand.

The priest put up his hand to stop the laughter. "Tell us about tonight's sermon, my son. Some of our friends think that you are boasting."

John was not boasting. He repeated the priest's words exactly as he had said them and with the same gestures. John was able to imitate jugglers and show people. He could imitate a fine speaker just as well.

When he had finished the people who had scoffed at him were silent. Later they talked about the way he had repeated the whole sermon.

When they were alone the priest said to John, "You have a very good memory, my son. What is your name?"

"My name is John, Father. John Bosco. I live in the village of Becchi."

"Do you go to school?" asked the priest.

"No, Father", John replied. "We can't afford that. My father is dead. My mother works very hard just for the food we eat and the clothes we wear."

"How many brothers and sisters do you have, John?" The priest was kind in his questions and so interested that John told him all about his home life.

"Would you like to go to school, John?" he asked.

"Oh, Father, more than anything else in the world," said John, "except for one thing."

"And what is that?"

"I'd like to be a priest more than anything else in the world." The boy said it so firmly that the priest knew he must have been thinking about it for a long time.

"You couldn't be a priest without a great deal of schooling, John."

"I know", John said sadly. "That's why I wish I could go to school."

"Well, who knows?" The priest seemed to be thinking aloud. "Perhaps something might be arranged." He smiled at the boy. "You go along home and tell your mother to come to see me tomorrow. Tell her that my name is Don Calosso. Maybe we'll have some good news for you."

It was indeed good news that John's mother brought back to him the next day.

"Johnny! Johnny!" she called excitedly as she came in the door. "I've been to see Don Calosso at the church. He wants you to come to him every morning."

"To work for him? Oh, Mother, to work for a priest?" The happiness in the boy's eyes was good to see.

"No, Johnny," said his mother, "not to work for him but to work with him. He is going to teach you."

"Do you mean that I am to go to school to him? But we can't pay for that." His joy was gone. He couldn't hide his disappointment.

"We can't pay for it with money, John, but you can pay by being a good student. You can pay by becoming a good and holy man because of the lessons that Don Calosso will teach you."

"Oh, Mother, can I really go?" He could hardly believe his good fortune. "But what about the work here? How will you manage?"

"We'll manage somehow, Johnny", said his mother. "This chance for you to learn is surely a gift from God. We must make the most of it."

Although he was very busy with his parish duties and quite old, Don Calosso enjoyed teaching his new student. John was so eager to learn that it was a pleasure to teach him. The boy worked hard at his lessons. Grammar and Latin meant a great deal to him. He knew that as a priest he would have a special need for these subjects.

"Don Calosso is so kind and patient, Mother." John looked up from the homework he was doing at the kitchen table. "He never loses his temper. You know, when I'm a priest, I want to be just like him."

"Why is that, Johnny?" asked his mother.

"He's very holy, Mother, but not a bit solemn. He always seems so happy and peaceful. He works hard for the people of his parish but he's never too busy nor in too much of a hurry to be kind, especially to the children. They run to him whenever they see him. No one is the least bit afraid of him. You can see that he loves everyone, and you just know that he loves God. He truly lives like our Lord."

"All priests try to live like our Lord, Johnny", his mother said.

"I know", John replied thoughtfully. "But not all priests have Don Calosso's ways. He is the one I shall copy", he said, turning back to his lessons.

No matter how late John had to stay up to finish his homework, he was always up early in the morning. He had to do a day's work at home before he left for school.

Joseph was always helping him, but not Anthony. He wasn't at all pleased about John's schooling.

"Why does he need book learning?" he demanded. "I'm much older than he, and I never had any. I'm a good farmer without such nonsense. That's just his lazy way of getting out of the work that has to be done around here."

"You know very well that he does his share of the work", his mother replied. "How can you say that he's lazy when he's up before dawn to do his work and half of yours?"

"Oh, you always stand up for him", Anthony said angrily. "You're only my step-mother, and you certainly act the part."

"How dare you say that!" John shouted. "You know very well that Mother does as much for you as she does for Joseph and me. She really does more because she has always tried to make up for the mother who died when you were a little boy."

"Hear him! Hear the fancy words of the student." Anthony struck out at John, ready to knock him down.

"Stop it, Anthony." Margaret Bosco sprang between the two boys. "I'll have no more of this. You're too big for such ways. Our home should be a peaceful, happy place. You make it a battlefield with your bitter words."

"I don't like this any more than you do", Anthony replied frowning. "But I don't intend to change my ways. John must give up his schooling. I'm the oldest son. I'm the boss around here."

The struggle went on for almost a year. In spite of this great trouble, John kept on doing well in his lessons. He was up early each morning to do his work. Then, without breakfast, he walked the three miles to serve Mass for Don Calosso and to receive our Lord daily.

Anthony's anger became more and more frightening. Margaret Bosco was afraid that her stepson would try to harm John. It was clearly necessary to keep the two boys apart.

"If you are to keep on with your studies, John, you will have to go away", she stated sadly. "It's no longer safe for you to be in the same house with Anthony. His jealousy and anger may cause him to harm you."

Her tears fell as she packed her youngest son's clothing. "If only there were some other way! I've tried and tried but I can't think of anything else to do. You must go to Moncucco, John. It's far enough away from here. There are many farms in that district. Our Lady will surely help you to find work."

"But my lessons!" John could hardly keep back his tears.

"You have your books with you. I packed them with your clothes. Study whenever you can. Maybe Anthony will change his ways while you are gone. Then you can return and go on with your lessons with Don Calosso. Go, my son, and God go with you."

It was a sad parting, but both John and his mother knew that it was necessary. He left quickly to keep from meeting Anthony. There was not even time to say good-bye to Don Calosso.

The road to Moncucco was long and tiring. John stopped many times to ask for work or to rest.

No one in the towns and villages needed help, so he kept on into the country.

At last he reached Moncucco and inquired at each farm. It was a cold February. They would not begin to hire until spring. Everywhere he went, he heard the same story: "Come back at the end of March. We'll be hiring farm help then."

It began to look hopeless. John couldn't wait until spring. He needed work now. His small bundle of clothes and his few books grew heavier and heavier. He decided to try just one more place. He stopped at a farm that belonged to a man named Moglia.

"No, we can't use any help right now", the farmer said. "But you may rest for a while. Come in. You look tired, my boy. Where are you from?"

"My home is in Becchi," replied John, "on the other side of Castlenuova."

"That is quite far away", the farmer remarked. "I knew a man who lived there some years ago. His name was Bosco, Francis Bosco. He did some work for me one summer."

"That must have been a long time ago, Mr. Moglia", said John. "Francis Bosco was my father. He has been dead almost twelve years, God rest him. My two brothers and I take care of the farm for my mother. Times are not good now. That is why I am looking for work."

Mr. Moglia looked at the boy carefully. "I'm not sure that you can do the heavy work that needs to be done around here, but I remember your father very well. He was a good man and a good worker. You may stay because of him."

"Oh, thank you, sir. I'll do my very best. You won't be sorry that you hired me."

Mr. Moglia took John into his home because he felt sorry for him. He didn't really expect very much work from the boy, but he soon found out that he had hired an unusually good worker.

The Moglia farm was a large one. The work there was very much like the work John had done at home, but there was a great deal more of it. He had very little time for himself. In fact, he had to study while he took care of the sheep and cattle.

He always carried one of his books in his pocket or tucked one into his shirt. While the sheep and cattle grazed in the pasture, John studied his Latin and grammar. He had made up his mind not to forget anything that Don Calosso had taught him.

On Sundays he was free to do whatever he liked. Then he would gather boys and girls around him. The news of his tricks and his wonderful stories soon spread. Each Sunday young people came from the farms to see his shows.

Most of these children knew as little about their religion as the children in Castlenuova. John interested these boys and girls first with his shows and then with his teaching.

He had been with the Moglia family about a year when early one morning on his way to water the cattle, he saw a stranger enter the yard. As the man walked toward him, he waved and called out, "John, John Bosco. Don't you know me?"

As the man came nearer, John saw that it was his Uncle Michael. He quickly set down the water buckets and ran toward him.

"Is anything wrong at home? How is Mother?" he asked excitedly.

"Don't look so frightened, John. Your mother is well and sends you her love. There's nothing wrong at home. I happened to be coming this way on business and thought that I would stop and see how things are with you. Do you like it here?" he asked kindly.

For a moment John didn't answer. Then he said slowly, "Yes, I like it here. The people I work for are very good, and they have been so kind to me. But I do wish that I could go home. I'm afraid I'll soon forget all that Don Calosso taught me. And if I stay away much longer, I'll be too old to go to school."

"Johnny, you're going home right now", declared Uncle Michael. "Water the cattle while I talk to Mr. Moglia. When you finish, pack your belongings. Then as soon as you've said good-bye, we'll be on our way to Becchi."

It didn't take John long to carry out his uncle's orders. He thanked Mr. Moglia for all his kindness and was soon on his way home.

When he came home, there was much rejoicing.

His mother welcomed him with tears of happiness, and Joseph wouldn't let him out of sight.

But Anthony did not show any pleasure at seeing him. He hadn't changed at all since John went away. His first words of greeting were, "I hope there'll be no more nonsense about schoolbooks."

"Can't you even wait until tomorrow to talk about that?" his mother asked anxiously. "Please, Anthony, let's not have any unpleasantness on John's first night home."

"First night or second night, it's all the same to me", he replied crossly. "I forbid John to open those foolish books."

"That's not for you to say, Anthony", his mother said quietly. "This is my house as well as yours. Let's have no more of that kind of talk."

"There's one way to end that kind of talk, as you call it", Anthony shouted angrily. "Give me my share of what my father left. Then I'll go off and find some place of my own."

There was a shocked silence in the little room.

"If that's the way you want it, Anthony, I'll be glad to give you your share. You know, of course, that there is very little to divide. But whatever there is, you shall have your share."

As soon as his share was agreed upon, Anthony started looking for a small farm of his own where he could run things to suit himself. He took with him a few chickens, some sheep, and a cow.

With Anthony away and happy in his own house, peace returned to the home of Margaret Bosco and her other two sons.

Soon after his return to Becchi John went to see his good friend and teacher, Don Calosso. The priest welcomed him with honest pleasure.

"You are able to study with me again?" he asked eagerly.

"Yes, Father, I am, if you will have me", the boy replied. "Things are much better at home."

"They are with me too," the priest said, "at least in one way. In another they are not so good."

John looked troubled.

"Don't worry, my son. It's just that I'm getting old. My health is not as good as it was. Much of my work is now being done by younger priests."

He sighed, and John understood that the saintly man didn't want to give up any of his services for God.

"Well, who knows?" Don Calosso added after a moment of thought. "Maybe this is all part of God's good plan. With less parish work I shall have more time to spend teaching you."

"Will that not tire you, Father?" John asked anxiously.

"No, no, my son", said Don Calosso. "Teaching you will rest my heart and soul."

"Can I be of some help to you, Father?" asked John. "I could take care of your fire and clean for you. I can cook too. I'd be so glad if I could do something to show you how grateful I am for your teaching."

"Now that's a good idea." The priest was pleased. He knew that John valued the lessons, but it was good to hear him say so. "With you to take care of my household chores, I shall have more time and strength for teaching. I'd like to have you come and stay with me, John. Do you think your mother can spare you?"

"I'm quite sure she can, Father. My brother Joseph will help her all he can. He often does my share of the work so that I can get on with my studies."

"Doesn't he want to study, too?" the priest asked.

John smiled. It was hard to picture Joseph with a book. "No, Father. Joseph likes to think of me as a priest. He will do anything he can to help me become one. But as for himself", he hesitated. "Well, it's like my tumbling and juggling tricks. My brother likes to watch them, but he has no desire to do them himself."

So it was decided that John would live at Don Calosso's house. He began his lessons where he had left off.

"You have not forgotten anything that I taught you", said the old priest. "Thank God for giving you such a good mind. Try always to use it for him."

John was sure that he would. It looked now as

if he were really on his way toward his life's purpose.

Living under the same roof with the priest was good for John. He did well with his lessons, and he learned a great deal about holiness. Don Calosso's good example was always before his eyes.

One afternoon when John's work was finished, Don Calosso said, "Take the rest of the day off, my son. It's time you went to visit your mother."

"You are sure you don't need me, Father?" asked John.

"No, no. Go along. Come back in the morning."

John had just entered the cottage when he heard someone running up the path and calling as he ran, "John, John Bosco. Come quickly. Father has been taken sick. He needs you."

John fairly flew over the road back to Don Calosso whom he had just left in good health. When he reached his good friend, he could hardly believe what he saw. The priest was lying on his bed, white and still.

"He must be dead", John thought as he hurried across the room to him.

Don Calosso was not dead. He was still alive and knew what was going on, but he could not speak. He'd had a stroke.

He motioned to John to take something from under his pillow. John reached for it and held up a key. The priest made signs for John to open his desk. The boy did so at once. He found a box and carried it to the bed. Don Calosso made John know that he wanted him to keep it. Then the tired old priest closed his eyes. He had gone home to God to receive the reward he had earned so well.

Relatives and friends came to pay their last respects. The whole village was at the funeral Mass. When it was over, John returned home.

He wept at the death of his dearest friend. He would miss him more than anyone could ever know. Then too he was troubled about his studies. He could not pay for his schooling. How could he keep on learning without Don Calosso?

He looked at the box that was his friend's last gift to him. He touched it gently as if it were the priest's own hand. When he opened it, he found a large sum of money.

John counted it. "Why, there is enough here to pay for all the schooling I need to become a priest. That is what Don Calosso meant when he sent me to open his desk. It must have taken him a long time to save all this."

For a moment all John's troubles were over—but only for a moment.

"He never spent a penny for himself", thought John as his tears fell on the box.

He remembered the well-worn cassock and the patched shoes of his teacher.

"I can't keep this for myself", he said. "It should go to Don Calosso's family. His relatives should have it. He helped them while he lived. They will need money more than ever now that he is gone. I'll take it to them at once."

He returned home a short time later, empty-handed.

"What shall I do now about my schooling?" he wondered. "How shall I ever become a priest?"

Once again, his mother found a way for him.

"John," she said, "I think we can arrange for you to attend the Latin classes in the free school at Castlenuova."

"But, Mother, even if the lessons are free, I'd need to pay for books and food as well as a few clothes", said John. "We haven't enough money for that."

"Never mind the money", his mother replied. "We'll find a way to take care of that. The distance to Castlenuova is another thing. You'd have to leave here very early in the morning and come home at noon. Then you'd have to return for the afternoon classes and come home again for supper. That's three miles each way, Johnny. Can you do it?"

"Oh, Mother, just give me the chance. I'd walk all those miles barefoot every day if only I could become a priest."

His mother smiled at his eagerness. She knew how much this meant to her son. She knew how much this meant to her. He must have his chance.

CHAPTER FOUR

J OHN'S SCHOOL DAYS at Castlenuova did not turn
out to be happy ones. His cheap, ill-fitting
clothes caused great merriment among his classmates. He didn't mind that, but when his teachers
refused to read and correct his papers he became
discouraged.

"A stupid peasant boy from the farm country
can't keep up with the work we do here", they
said. "You'd better go back to your sheep and
cows."

"Please give me a chance to show you what I
can do", John begged.

Finally they did, but not willingly. Only the boy's strong will kept him from giving up and returning home.

The students were cruel, and the teachers unjust. But he could stand all their unkindness if only he would be allowed to stay and learn. Finally he did convince one of his teachers to read some of his written work.

"Your papers are perfect, my farmer friend." There was insult in the man's voice. "In fact, they are so perfect that they couldn't possibly be your work. You must have copied from a book or from some other boy. It looks as if you cheated. You'd better admit it."

But no boy in the whole school was smart enough to do such good work. No book could be found from which John could have copied. Still it took a great deal of time and patience for the "stupid peasant boy" to make the teachers believe that the work was his own.

It was an unhappy year for John, but he learned a great deal that was useful to him in later years.

"I'll never let any boys I teach suffer the way I have", he decided. "I'll be patient and kind with them. I'll let them talk to me and explain so that they won't be punished unjustly."

There were other hardships that year. When cold weather came, John had to give up the long walks to and from school. His thin, worn clothes couldn't keep out the wintry winds. He had to find a place to stay in Castlenuova.

He found room and board in the home of a tailor who lived not far from the school.

"You may help me in my shop to pay for your room", the tailor said. "But I'll have to have money to pay for the food you eat."

"I'm sorry but I haven't any money for that", John said. "Would you be willing to accept produce from our farm instead?"

"Indeed I'd be most willing", the tailor agreed. "Who wouldn't accept fresh eggs from the country? Maybe you can get some grain for me. I can grind that into flour for our bread. But how can the food be brought to me?"

"My mother will bring it here each week when she comes to market", John told him. "And I'll ask her to bring you some of her good homemade cheese to eat with the bread you bake."

The tailor smiled. "You've made your plans to stay with me. Well, I'm pleased to have you. It should be good for both of us."

It turned out to be just that. John worked hard for the tailor. Before long he could cut and sew men's clothes as well as mend and press them.

Robert, the tailor, was also Robert, the musician. He played the violin and piano and sang in the choir. One day while he was practicing, John sang along with him.

"I didn't know that you could sing", Robert exclaimed in surprise. "You have a good voice. We need fellows like you in our choir. Come along with me tonight and try out for it."

The choirmaster was greatly pleased with the boy's voice. He invited him to become a member. Very soon John Bosco was able to sing God's praises in the church. He loved music, and his friend enjoyed teaching him about it. It was hard to say which of the two was more pleased when John could both sing and play.

John practiced whenever he could spare a few minutes from all the work he had to do. He didn't know it then, but his tailoring and the music would someday be among the most valuable lessons he ever learned.

The school year ended at last, and John returned home for three months. He was quite downhearted, for he thought that his year at the Latin school had been almost wasted. If his next school year was as disappointing as this one, how could he ever go on to be a priest?

His mother noticed that he didn't go about the farm work in his usual cheery way. She was worried about him, but she didn't ask any questions.

One morning he came to breakfast whistling happily. His sadness was gone. Then his mother did question him.

"What makes you so happy this morning, Johnny?" She placed a bowl of hot meal in front of him. "You've been so quiet and sad ever since you came home. What has changed you?"

"A dream has changed me, mother", he replied with a smile. "A strange and wonderful dream like the one I had a long time ago. Remember?"

"Of course, I do", she said. "That was when you told me you wanted to be a priest."

"Yes, I knew that I wanted to be a priest, but lately I've been wondering how I could ever become one. I shall not worry about that any more. I know now that I am to be a priest", he declared.

"How can you be so certain now, Johnny," asked his mother, "when yesterday you were not at all sure?"

"It was the dream, Mother. That is what makes me certain. It was no ordinary dream. It was like the other one. The same beautiful lady was in this one too. She came toward me leading a large flock of sheep and lambs. She called me by name, saying, 'Come, John, I'm putting this flock in your charge.'

" 'But what can I do with them, dear lady', I said to her. 'I have no pasture.'

" 'Don't be afraid', she replied. 'I will look after you and help you.'

"Then she was gone. You see, Mother, I no longer need to worry. A way will be found for me to become a priest."

All during the vacation months, Margaret Bosco tried to find some way for John to go ahead with his schooling. He hadn't been able to progress as he should at Castlenuova. He must go some place where he could really advance.

If only she could manage to send him to the state school at Chieri. There he would be taught Greek as well as Latin. There he would be taught all of the things he would need to learn before he could train for the priesthood. Perhaps the farm products would help pay the tuition. They'd have to find out.

John too was trying to make plans for the fall.

"If only there were some way for me to earn money this summer", he said. "Even a little would help with my tuition."

"You can't earn money while you are working on our farm", his mother replied. "So don't trouble yourself about that. We need your help here and maybe the farm will help you. The grain that you are growing, the grapes that are ripening will quite likely take the place of money. Maybe they can be used to pay for books and some of the things that you need."

"That's true, Mother", he smiled at her. "I wish that you did not have to make so many sacrifices for me. You are so good to me. What would I ever do without you? I am very thankful to the dear Lord for you."

John's mother put her arm around his shoulder. "I'm very thankful to the dear Lord too. I'm thankful that he lets me help in his plan for you to become a priest."

School began early in November. When the time came, John once more left home. This time he was loaded down with a huge bag of grain which he carried on his back. Beautiful purple grapes filled two baskets which he carried, one in each hand.

Chieri was twelve miles from Becchi, and he had to travel the whole way on foot. He stopped at the marketplace at Castlenuova. There he sold the grain and the grapes at a good price. He used the money to buy pens and paper and other school supplies that he would need. Then he went on to the state school.

He was enrolled at once. The next thing was to find a place to live while he was going to school. Someone told him of a Madam Matta, a woman of wealth who needed a servant. He hurried to her house and was invited in to talk to her.

"I've come to ask for work as a servant", he said eagerly.

"Have you a reference from your last place?" Madam Matta asked.

"I have a letter from my pastor. He will tell you that I am honest", he answered.

"I feel sure that you are", she said. "But how can I be certain that you can do the work that I need?"

"If you will just give me a chance, I'm sure you will not be disappointed", John replied.

"Well, you may bring your belongings as soon as you wish", she said.

"I have them with me", he answered quickly. "May I begin work now?"

Madam Matta smiled at his eagerness. "Come, I will show you to your room."

On the way through the long hall and up the

winding stairs to the attic, John told her about school. "I will have to do the cleaning and scrubbing early in the morning and late at night. I'll fit the work in with my classes. I promise I will not neglect anything you want done", he assured her.

"No, I can see that you are not the kind that would", she said. "However, I didn't know that you were a student."

John's heart fell. Maybe he wasn't to have the job after all.

"I have a young son who does poorly in his lessons. He needs help from an older student. Do you think you can find time for helping him too?" Madam Matta asked.

"I'll be glad to teach your boy. I'll enjoy that very much, and it will be good training for me. You see, I want to spend my life teaching boys when I have finished my schooling."

John Bosco spent two years in the home of Madam Matta. He left only when her son had finished his education.

John's next job was quite different. This time he found work in a bakery. He had to scrub and sweep the floors. He had to wash mixing bowls and spoons and keep the baking pans spotless. Most of all he enjoyed watching the baker turn out crisp, brown loaves of bread. Before long he had learned to bake almost as well as the owner himself. He became so good at his job that the baker offered to make him a partner.

"You'll be rich, John", he said. "Very rich! You won't need to work for your board and room. You'll be able to buy yourself a fine house. Maybe you can even hire servants", he urged.

"No, no", John replied without hesitation. "Thank you, my friend, for your generous offer, but I have chosen my life's work. I will not turn away from it."

John slept in a small, cold corner under the stairs at the baker's shop. It was a miserable place, and his bed was most uncomfortable. He seldom had a good night's sleep there. He stayed up as late as he could and got up very early. He didn't want to spend any more time there than he had to.

Since he spent only a few hours sleeping, he had more time for his homework. When he finished his lessons, he spent the rest of the night writing. Words came easily to him, and he practiced writing essays, letters, and even stories. He didn't write them for any particular purpose, but without knowing it, John Bosco was training himself for one of his most important works.

Someday he would be not only a teacher of boys but also a famous writer and speaker. Everything that John Bosco did or learned was a step forward toward his great purpose.

John was happy at Chieri. He learned so quickly that he was able to do two years' work in one.

His classmates were quite different from the boys who had made life miserable for him at the school at Castlenuova. Now his outstanding work brought admiration and respect. His happy spirit brought friendships. No one scoffed at his poor clothes. His schoolmates understood. They admired him for working under such hardships to get an education.

John was a big fellow and a strong one. He had a hearty appetite and not always enough food to satisfy it. When his friends discovered this, they shared their own lunches with him. They were tactful about this, for they knew that John was proud. John gratefully accepted their gifts, and he never forgot their kindness.

One morning John arrived late for one of his classes. His work at the bake shop had delayed him. In his hurry he had forgotten his most important book. It was a book written in Latin, telling the life story of a famous Roman. The students had to read it in class and translate it into Italian as they read.

John arrived just in time for his turn to read. He was afraid to say that he had forgotten his book. He would be given a very low mark for that. Instead he picked up another book and pretended to read and translate from it.

John was getting along very well indeed until one of the boys near him discovered that he was reading from the wrong book. Not only that, but he was holding it upside down! He nudged the boy next to him.

"Look what Bosco is doing", he whispered.

The word was passed along. One after another turned to see John translating perfectly from the wrong book, which he was holding upside down! The class began to laugh.

"What is all this merriment about?" the teacher asked. He was very much annoyed at the laughter. "Stop this nonsense at once. John Bosco, repeat that last paragraph."

John did, word for word, just as he had the first time.

The boys clapped their hands and shouted, "Bravo! Bravo! What a student!"

"Silence", shouted the teacher. "Will someone kindly explain what is going on here?"

One boy spoke up. "It's Bosco, sir. He doesn't have the Latin book with him, but he has given a perfect translation without it."

The teacher strode to the back of the room, picked up the book, and looked at it carefully. There were no papers in it, no notes for John to follow.

"Amazing!" exclaimed the teacher. "You have done the impossible! You deserve the cheers of your classmates. I add my own. However, in the future you must use the right textbook. God has blessed you with a wonderful mind and a most unusual memory. Always use them for God's purpose."

School days were busy ones for John, but on Sundays he was free to do as he pleased. In his walks about the town he met many young people.

Some roamed the streets with nothing to do. Some got themselves into trouble.

Here was work for him. He would spend his free hours with these boys. Perhaps he could teach them to put their time to better use.

He began by making friends with one or two, then with a few more. Some of the boys tried to talk John into gambling and stealing as they did. It didn't take them long to find out that this could not be done. Either they changed their ways for the better or they left their new friend to go back to their evil doings.

Most of the boys liked John Bosco. He was a big fellow for eighteen, and he commanded their respect, not only for his size but his friendly manner. They enjoyed his magic tricks and his good stories. One told another about him, and his group grew rapidly.

One Sunday as they sat on the grass in the town park, he said to them, "We have enough boys to form a club. How would you like that?"

There were loud cheers. "A club! That's just the thing. Let's have a club. What shall we name it?"

Of course there were many ideas for a name, some good and some silly. John stopped them all.

"Let's not talk about a name until we have some rules", he said.

"Make it just a few then", shouted the boys. "We don't want many rules."

"We'll not have many", John agreed with a smile.

He knew all too well that these boys weren't used to obeying rules or laws either. "I'll promise you that we'll have just a few important rules. In fact, two will be enough."

"What are they?" demanded the boys. "We'll have to hear them first. If they don't please us, we'll not agree to keep them."

"Well here they are, fellows", said John. "If there's one among you who thinks he can't keep them, let me know.

"First: No member of our club will do anything that a child of God should not do.

"Second: Be cheerful about everything you do."

John saw the boys looking at each other. What sort of rules were these? He didn't wait for anyone to ask the questions. He began at once to explain them.

"I'll begin our meetings with some stories about God. In them I'll tell you what he expects of his children. There are certain things that our Lord expects of everyone."

"Like what?" one boy asked. "I'm a schoolboy. What does he expect of me?"

"If you are a schoolboy you are expected to study your lessons. Our Lord expects you to obey your teachers and to do your work honestly."

"I work for my living. What's expected of me?" There was a sneer in the voice of the big, awkward fellow who asked that question.

"If you work for a living, work hard", John

Bosco replied patiently. "Try to please the man you work for. Give him an honest day's labor for the pay he gives you."

"They don't pay us much", two or three called out.

"Maybe they are giving you all that they can. Even if they aren't, God expects you to do a little more than you are paid for—never any less."

These were strange words to most of these boys. Practically all of them tried to get by with doing as little as possible, whether they went to school or worked for their living.

"We'll give it a try", shouted one. The rest decided to follow their leader.

"Good! That's what I had hoped to hear", John said. "Now we can name the club. I know that we're going to have fun together. I know you're all going to feel good when you realize that you are doing what is right. You'll be a happy crowd."

"How about calling our club the *Happy Company?*" one boy suggested.

"That's a fine idea." John was pleased with the name. "From now on we'll be called the Happy Company."

That is the way John Bosco's first Happy Company began many, many years ago. Later there would be boys' clubs bearing that name all over the world. For that little group in the town of Chieri marked the beginning of one of John Bosco's greatest works.

CHAPTER FIVE

THE HAPPY COMPANY met each Sunday, not always in the same place but wherever a meeting place could be found. Sometimes they went on hikes into the country. There they picked wild berries or climbed trees or played games. Sometimes they ran races or jumped over streams using up their boyish energy in a wholesome way.

When they were tired out, they'd lie down in the deep grass and rest. Then John Bosco would tell them the stories they loved to hear.

Many of his stories were about God and the

Blessed Mother. He also told true and exciting stories of saints who had fought against the devil. He told of angels who had fallen from God's grace and of other angels who forever sang his praise. He taught them the truths of their religion and showed them how to practice what he taught.

The day's outing always began with Mass and ended with a visit to some church for vespers and Benediction. Then the boys would go their separate ways. After these meetings they felt better able to do the hard work ahead of them. They were better able to face the miseries of their poor homes and the trials of their daily lives.

One Sunday as they came near a large church in the center of the town, they noticed a big crowd outside. There were very few people going into the church. They were laughing and shouting. They seemed to be enjoying whatever was going on.

A few of the boys elbowed their way into the middle of the crowd and then pushed their way out to tell the others what they had seen.

"It's an acrobat", one said. "He's putting on a fine show. Let's not go to church. Let's stay out with the rest of the crowd and watch him."

"Oh, he's not so good", another said. "Our own John can do as well as that."

"Maybe so", said another. "But it would be fun to watch this fellow. Come on. Let's go."

By this time John Bosco had caught up with his boys. At once he saw what was happening.

"Tell you what, boys," he said. "We'll all go into church as we had planned. But before we go in, I'll talk to this performer. If he will meet us some night after work, I'll bet him that I can top anything he can do."

"Yeah", the cry went up from the Happy Company. "How about that, Mr. Acrobat?"

"How much will you bet?" the showman asked. "It will have to be worthwhile before I'll agree."

He really didn't want to make this bet with John. If he lost, he would lose his name as a good showman. People would make fun of him. He'd no longer be able to attract the big crowds in front of the church. Still, a contest with this big fellow might be an easy way to win some money.

John Bosco could see what the man was thinking. "If you win, I'll give you as much money as you earn in a week", he promised.

John had no idea where that much money would come from, but he felt sure he wouldn't have to pay it. He was almost sure he could win. There was so much more at stake than money. The man was keeping people from going into church. Even his own boys were tempted to stay outside and watch instead of going inside to Mass. If he beat the performer at his own tricks, the fellow would be ashamed to come there again.

"Very well, that's a bet", said the acrobat. "I'll meet you, but you're bound to lose."

The time came for the contest. John and his boys hurried to the park across from the church. This was to be the meeting place. There was the acrobat waiting for them.

"What's first on the program?" he asked with a sneer. He thought that all this was a waste of time, but he was willing to go along with it for the sake of the money he'd win.

"You name it, and I'll do it", replied John. He too was very sure of himself.

This was all very exciting to the Happy Company. They knew that their leader was good. But was he that good?

"How about a race?" asked the showman. "Say from here to the edge of the city?"

"That's quite a way, but I'm willing", John agreed.

The boys stepped back. The two men lined up.

"On your mark. Get set. Go!"

Each runner was off like a streak. Both were good, but at first the showman was in the lead.

"Faster, faster, John", shouted his boys, running along after them. "Don't let him beat you. Faster!"

John pushed himself a bit more. He caught up with the other runner and stayed with him for a short distance. Then with a sudden spurt he was far ahead. He crossed the finish line, turned around, and waited for the showman.

A great cheer went up from his loyal boys.

"The winner", they shouted as they crowded around him. They were very pleased that their John had won.

The other runner was not at all pleased. "You beat me in the race", he said. "But I'm a little out of practice. How about jumping?"

"Whatever you say", John agreed cheerfully.

"How much do you bet this time?" asked the acrobat.

"I'll double it", said John. "Just name the place."

"We'll jump across the river. Down near the bridge, there's a good place."

Off they went, the acrobat leading the way and John and his boys hurrying after him.

The river was narrow at the spot the man had chosen, but there was a low wall on the opposite side. This was going to be hard.

"Go ahead", John said to the showman. "Jump!"

And jump he did. He landed gracefully on both feet on the opposite side of the river.

John's boys looked at each other. They began searching their pockets. They'd each have to give what little money they had. It was plain to see who'd win that bet.

"I can't let them pay", John was thinking.

He measured the distance across the flowing water with his eye. He took his place at the water's edge. With a flying leap he was across! He landed on a ledge of the wall a short distance beyond his opponent.

"Bravo! Bravo!" The cheers of the Happy Company were deafening.

John had a broad grin on his face as he crossed the bridge and returned to the other side. The other jumper looked angry and downhearted.

"How about trying something else, my friend?" John felt sorry for the fellow.

The man brightened. "You double the bet again, and I'll do a juggling trick."

"Agreed", John said without hesitating. "But this time I'll go first."

John looked around and found a straight stick on the ground. He smoothed it off with his knife. Then he twirled it around a few times to test it.

The boys gathered around open-mouthed. Now what was he going to do? Here was a trick they'd never seen.

John balanced the twirling stick on the palm of his hand and then on the tips of his fingers. While it was still spinning, he balanced it on his elbow, shoulder, chin, mouth, nose, and head. Then he did the whole thing in reverse. He ended his show with a bow.

This time the boys were speechless. They could hardly believe their eyes. They'd never seen anything like that before.

The juggler had. This would be easy for him. After all didn't he earn his living doing tricks like that? He'd show them this time!

He picked up the stick and did very well until

he got it near his nose which was large and rather crooked. The stick bumped against it and fell to the ground.

But the contest was not over. The showman was not ready to give up. He had made up his mind to beat John Bosco, and also he wanted to win the money.

John admired the fellow's will to win. He was willing to make another try, but he too had made up his mind to win—not for the sake of winning nor for the money but to keep the man away from the church door on Sundays.

"This will be a tree-climbing contest", the defeated juggler announced in his best showman's manner.

"Agreed", John Bosco replied.

The showman swung himself up on a low-hanging branch of a nearby tree. Up, up he went, hand over hand, until he reached the top.

"Well done", shouted the boys admiringly.

Then down he came quite pleased with himself.

"Up you go, young fellow", he said good-naturedly. "Beat me if you can."

John grabbed hold of a low branch and swung himself on up, just as his opponent had done. Up, up he went, hand over hand until he reached the top.

That was a tie. The boys held their breath. What more could he do? There was no way to climb higher.

But John Bosco did go higher and without climbing. There at the top of the tree, he stood on his hands with his two feet waving high above the tree! Once more he had won.

The shouting and clapping could be heard for miles. When John reached the ground, his boys picked him up and carried him around on their shoulders. They slapped his back and shook his hands. He was truly their hero.

John pushed his way out of the shouting, cheering crowd. He walked over to the man he had defeated.

"You admit that I am the winner?" he asked.

"I do indeed, sir." The poor fellow looked most unhappy. For one thing he could no longer gather a crowd outside the church on Sundays. The people would laugh at him since he had been defeated in this contest. For another, he didn't have the money to pay his bet. He was feeling very low.

John stood quietly watching him. He could see that the man had learned his lesson. He shook his hand in a friendly way.

"I'll not collect the money you owe me", he said. "Instead you can treat these boys to a good spaghetti dinner."

The man's face brightened. The dinners wouldn't cost nearly the amount of the bet.

"Very good, very good!" he said. "Come along, all of you. There's an inn just down the road."

"Wait," John said, "one more thing before you go. I want you to promise me that you will not keep people from going to Mass on Sundays."

"I'll gladly promise that." The man was greatly

relieved. He grabbed John's hand and shook it. "In fact, I'll do more than that. I'll go to church myself. Now come along my friends. We're all hungry after this day's show."

Off they all went, the juggler, John Bosco, and his Happy Company, to laugh and talk and share a good meal. Now they were all friends. The winnings and losses of the day were forgotten.

CHAPTER SIX

Hıs Sunday outings with the poor boys of Chieri took a great deal of John Bosco's time. But his lessons always came first. He knew that he must have the best possible education if he was to become a priest.

His boys all loved him, and he was devoted to them. They were all his friends, but he never singled out any one boy as his favorite. This was true among his schoolmates too. He was friendly with all of them but had no best friend until his last year at Chieri. This friendship was to make a lasting mark on him.

One morning at school the Latin teacher was late, very late. The boys grew restless waiting for him. One after another closed his textbook and began looking for something more exciting to do. Before long the room was in an uproar. The boys were behaving as most schoolboys do when there is no teacher to keep law and order.

John Bosco kept on reading. He didn't pay any attention to the others, and they didn't pay any attention to him. They were used to his quiet ways. But there was another boy who kept on with his studying. He was a new student, and no one knew very much about him.

Suddenly one noisy fellow caught sight of the new boy working away quietly. He was annoyed by the sight and began to throw pieces of chalk at him.

The quiet boy paid no attention but kept right on with his work. Then the bully began throwing books. Even this went unnoticed.

"What's the matter with you?" demanded the bully. "Are you too good to join in our fun?"

"Oh, no", the new boy answered. "It's just that I don't enjoy that sort of thing. I have a great deal of work to do, and I'd like to keep on with it."

"You'd better change your mind", was the bully's reply. "Are you with us or against us?"

"Of course I'm with you in other ways", the new student answered calmly. "But in this—well, I must keep on with my studying."

That was all the bully needed. He reached out and slapped the boy soundly on both cheeks.

The classroom was silent. The other boys held their breath and waited. Now there'd be a good fight. They all knew which one they hoped would win. But there was no fight.

The new boy stood up and spoke in a firm, fearless voice. "Now are you satisfied, my friend? You have done what you set out to do. Now will you let me go on with my work?"

The bully stared at him. Then strangely enough he walked away. The new boy picked up his book and went on reading as though nothing had happened.

John Bosco was greatly impressed. "Who is that boy?" he asked the student sitting next to him.

"Louis Comollo is his name", was the reply. "He has an uncle who is a very saintly priest."

"He must be just like his uncle judging by the way he took those blows", said John. "He wasn't afraid. He showed great spirit, but he didn't get angry. I admire that fellow. I'd like to know him."

John Bosco did get to know him. He and Louis Comollo became close friends. It was a rather strange friendship. John was a strong, eager young man, ready to rush into any adventure. He had never been able to overcome his hot temper completely, and he was always ready to fight for his friend.

But Louis would stop him, saying, "God doesn't

want you to use your strength for blows. You will be able to do more through kindness."

The first time Louis said that, John looked startled. He had heard those words before.

"Not with blows but with kindness . . ." The beautiful lady had said that to him in his dream when he was just a little boy.

John and Louis made a strange pair for Louis was the opposite of John in many ways. Louis preferred to read and write and do quiet things by himself. He didn't care a bit about mingling with the other boys.

But there was one strong interest the two boys shared. Both were deeply religious. Both had deep love for the Blessed Sacrament and the Mother of God.

Louis Comollo died when he was still a schoolboy at Chieri, but John Bosco never forgot him. Remembering Louis's ways helped John to change his headstrong spirit. When he became a teacher years later, the thought of Louis Comollo made him more patient in dealing with his own stupid or unruly students.

The Latin and Greek lessons finally came to an end. John Bosco's days as a schoolboy were over. Now the time had come for him to take the next step forward toward his life's purpose. This step would lead to his ordination as a priest of God.

Should he become a parish priest? Or should he become an order priest? He felt strongly drawn toward the Franciscans. Maybe it might be better if he became a Dominican or a Jesuit. There were so many things to think about. He must make the very best decision.

If he entered the seminary, it would be hard to find money for his expenses. He would no longer be able to work for his room and board, nor could he do odd jobs to pay for books and clothes. The subjects that he would have to study would take all of his time and every bit of his strength.

If he entered one of the monasteries, everything would be taken care of by the order of his choice. He didn't want to make the decision without good advice.

"Go to see Don Cafasso", one of his friends suggested. "He is a wise and understanding young priest and a very holy one. He will know how to direct you."

"Go into the seminary", Don Cafasso advised. "Go on with your studies. If God means for you to be a parish priest, he will take care of you. He will see that you get whatever money you need."

"Thank you, Father, for your helpful advice", said John. "I shall enter the seminary and put all my trust in God."

Almost at once, all of John Bosco's needs were taken care of in the most unexpected ways. Good friends gave him money for books and supplies. A kind priest paid his tuition. His old friend Robert, the tailor, made him a cassock. A shoemaker, for whom he had worked as a boy, supplied him with shoes.

Friends, neighbors, and relatives gave whatever they could to help the shepherd boy of Becchi become a priest.

Once inside the seminary, he soon won a scholarship. Then because of his good work, he was made sacristan of the seminary chapel. This job gave him a small salary which was a great help in paying for books and supplies.

His six years in the seminary were happy ones. Everyone was kind and helpful to him, but no one did more for the young student than Don Cafasso. He helped him in every way he could.

The years were long and the work was hard, but at last they came to an end. Part of his wonderful dream was about to come true. On June 5, 1841, John Bosco at the age of twenty-six was ordained a priest.

The ceremony took place in the chapel of Monsignor Fransoni, the archbishop of Turin. As he said the words, "Thou art a priest forever", John Bosco thought that he had never heard anything more beautiful. He had worked and prayed and waited for this great moment ever since he was a little boy. His wonderful dream was as clear to him now as it was on the morning he had told it to his mother.

He thought of her now in his great happiness. Next week he would go home to offer Mass at the little church in Becchi. Then he would give Holy Communion to his own mother. What greater joy could ever come to him?

His mother's pastor had invited him to return for his first Mass. There would be a feast in his honor. All the villagers as well as his friends and relatives would join in the celebration. He had decided that must wait. He wanted to offer his first Mass in Turin. He wanted to be alone with God and his Blessed Mother on that holy occasion.

"Thou art a priest forever." He repeated the words as he left the chapel. He could almost feel the archbishop's blessing upon him. Now he was Don Bosco, for in Italy *Don* means *Father*.

"I will be a father to the boys I teach. They will come to me with their troubles and their joys. I will be gentle and patient with them. I will help them know God. When they know him, they will love him as he wants to be loved."

Don Bosco woke early on the morning after his ordination.

"This is the day the Lord has made. Let us rejoice and be glad therein." The words of the psalm were in his heart the moment he opened his eyes. They never left him until he knelt at the foot of the altar in the Church of Saint Francis of Assisi, ready to begin his first Mass.

"I will go in to the altar of God, unto God who giveth joy to my youth."

Solemnly, reverently, and joyously he went forward toward the greatest moment in a young priest's life.

"The day before he suffered, he took bread . . . gave thanks . . . broke the bread, gave it to his disciples, and said: '. . . this is my Body.' "

The sacred time had come. His words and God's power brought down from heaven the Savior and Redeemer of all mankind.

Don Bosco held him up for all to see. Then he knelt again to adore. Only our Lord saw his tears of joy. Only God saw his thankful heart.

Then the Mass went on.

Knowing how generously God would answer his prayers offered at his first Mass, Don Bosco gave much reverent thought to the special favor he would ask. When the time came he knew exactly the favor he would ask. His boys were always first in his thoughts. He would ask God to give him the right words to carry his message to them.

"The young are so willing and eager to work for the things that they believe in", he prayed. "Let me teach them to believe in you. Let me have the gift to speak the words that will turn them from evil. Let me think and speak and write in a way that will bring souls to you."

Time has proved that Don Bosco's prayer was answered. Today he is known all over the world as one of the greatest speakers, teachers, and writers in his special field, boys.

CHAPTER SEVEN

S OON AFTER becoming a priest, Don Bosco was
given his choice of three places in which to
begin his work. It was hard to decide which one
to take. He was eager to begin parish work, but
he also wanted more education. This he could not
afford. He felt the need of advice, so he went to
Don Cafasso.

"Which place shall I choose?" he asked. "They
need a priest on one of the great estates in Genoa.
My own parish needs a young priest. In Castlenuova
one of the priests needs an assistant. Where can I
do the most good?"

"Do not accept any of these offers, John", Don Cafasso answered. "Instead, go to the Ecclesiastical College of Saint Francis de Sales here in Turin. You will be accepted because you have always been an outstanding student."

"I would love to have still more schooling", said John. "But the tuition? I couldn't possibly afford that. Wouldn't it be better for me to work in a parish? I would then have a small salary and could begin to repay those who have helped me, especially my mother."

"I'm sure your mother would be the last one to want you to do that", said Don Cafasso. "Her whole life has been to help you go forward in your work for God. If you study more, you will be able to do more."

"But my tuition?" John asked again.

"Don't worry about that", replied Don Cafasso. "The school has a fund for taking care of men like you. Come, I'll go with you while you register."

Don Bosco worked hard during the next three years. He studied and he wrote. He attended classes and he even taught a few classes. In his spare time he went with his friend Don Cafasso to visit the prisons and hospitals in Turin. On the way home the two priests would talk about the people they had just visited.

"Take those young boys locked up in jail for stealing apples", said John. "No doubt they would have bought the apples if they were not so poor. Their hunger tempted them too strongly."

"But John," said Don Cafasso, "stealing is a sin."

"Yes, yes, we both know that, but do those boys know it? No one ever taught them right from wrong. When they leave the prison, they'll be back in no time at all for the same crime. There must be a way to keep them from making their first mistake."

Don Bosco thought about this problem most of the time. What could be done for those poor boys?

On nights when he walked through the city, he saw them playing in the streets or hiding in the alleys—dirty, underfed boys, fighting, stealing, swearing children of all ages, doing wrong as naturally as well-cared-for children do what is right. No one loved these dead-end boys. No one wanted them. Something must be done about it, and soon.

One morning while Don Bosco was vesting for Mass, his prayers were suddenly interrupted. He was startled to hear running footsteps followed by angry shouts.

The priest hurried to the door. There stood a big fellow. His face and hands were dirty, and his hair looked as though it had never seen a comb. He put up his two hands to protect himself from the blows of the sacristan.

"Stop that at once", commanded Don Bosco. "What are you doing to the boy?"

"He won't serve your Mass, Father", the angry man replied. "The boy who was to serve is late. I thought this fellow could take his place."

"Well, if he doesn't want to serve my Mass, I'm sure he must have a good reason."

The priest turned to the frightened boy. "Have you a reason?" Don Bosco asked, smiling kindly.

"How can I serve Mass?" the boy replied sullenly. "I don't know the first thing about it."

"That's the best reason I know for not serving", said the priest.

"Then what was he doing back here?" demanded the man. "If he wasn't going to serve, he certainly doesn't belong here."

"I wasn't doing anything", mumbled the boy. "I just wanted to see what it was all about."

"Well, be off with you." The man again raised his hand as though to strike him.

Don Bosco stepped between the two. "No more of that", he said sternly. Then he put his arm across the boy's shoulder. "That's no way to treat a friend of mine."

"I'm sorry, Father", the man began to apologize. "I didn't know that he was a friend of yours. I didn't know that you even knew him."

"I didn't know him before today", Don Bosco replied. "But just as soon as anyone is treated badly, he at once becomes my friend. Go now and attend to your work. I want to talk to my young friend."

He turned to the boy. "What is your name?" he asked as soon as the sacristan had gone.

"Bartholomew Garelli", the boy answered. He was no longer frightened. Under Don Bosco's kind and interested questions, he soon told the priest all about himself. "My parents are dead, Father. I'm a bricklayer. That is how I earn my living when there is work."

"Can you read and write?" Don Bosco asked.

"No, Father", the boy replied. "I've never been to school, but I can sing. I can whistle too, better than any boy I know. Would you like to hear me, Father?"

"I would indeed," the priest replied, "but not now. It's time for Mass. Have you heard Mass today?"

"No", the boy answered, beginning to wonder whether he should have come here.

"Do you know anything about the catechism?" Don Bosco asked.

"Awhile back I went to catechism class, but there were just little kids in it. I was the only big one. I didn't like that. Besides the little ones knew more than I did."

"If I were to teach you your catechism, just you alone, would you want to learn?" asked the priest.

"Yes, I guess so", the boy replied. He liked the priest. He wouldn't mind learning the catechism to please him.

"Well, you wait here." Don Bosco led him to a chair near the door. "You can watch me offer Mass. When I get through, we can begin your lessons right away. Don't go away now." He smiled at the boy.

Don Bosco left him and went to offer Mass. "I will go in to the altar of God", he began.

"Bless this boy, dear Lord", he prayed. "Let me reach his heart. Let me turn his thoughts and deeds to you and the Blessed Mother."

Don Bosco did reach Bartholomew Garelli's heart that very day. A week later he returned for his second catechism lesson. With him he brought six of his friends. With this small group Don Bosco, their teacher, began the great Salesian Society, the society that would teach young people to become good and useful citizens in the eyes of God and man.

Each week more and more boys followed Bartholomew Garelli to Don Bosco's catechism class. As the group grew, the priest found that he needed a larger place to take care of all these boys.

"If only I could rent a room in the center of the town, I could take care of many more", he thought. But he knew he couldn't do that.

He was studying at the Ecclesiastical College and living there. He had no money of his own to pay rent for a room. He was troubled for he knew that there were many boys who needed his help.

Once more his good friend Don Cafasso advised

and helped him. He was now rector of the college.

"Bring your boys here on Sundays", he said. "There is a courtyard outside my bedroom window. You can teach them, and they can play games there. Then when it's time for benediction, you may bring them into the chapel."

"But the noise, Father", said Don Bosco. "It may bother you."

"No, it won't", Don Cafasso replied kindly. "The noise of happy children is a holy noise."

For the next three years the boys met in that courtyard. Each week a few more boys came to see what was going on. Usually they stayed to join. Most of them were young people who worked hard all day in the factories or the marketplace.

Some of them were little fellows only eight or nine years old. Some were big, overgrown boys of fifteen or sixteen. There were no child labor laws then, and many employers treated the boys unfairly. They were often so underpaid that they didn't have enough to eat. Very few of them had homes. Either their parents were dead or they came from evil families who wanted to be rid of their children.

These were the boys Don Bosco went looking for in the city of Turin. These were the boys who became members of his club. For them the Sunday meetings were the one bright spot in their hard lives. In a short time the group in the courtyard had grown to a hundred.

One Sunday there was quite a bit of whispering going on as the boys gathered. One of them had heard that their teacher was going to leave them to do parish work. There was great worry about the news. Would their good friend be sent to a distant city? If that happened, would it mean the end of their Sunday meetings?

Don Bosco himself thought about that possibility. But he didn't worry. The Blessed Mother had led him to these boys. She would surely take care of them.

The time came for the young priests to be told where they were to go. Don Bosco was finally called to the rector's office.

"I have just the place for you, John", Don Cafasso announced. "It is at Saint Philomena's Orphanage. They need a young priest. I believe you are the right man for the place. Don Borel, the priest in charge, agrees with me. He has arranged for you to have your boys there on Sundays. The orphanage is at Valdocco, just outside Turin. That is not too far for the boys to go for their meetings."

"How good you are, Father", Don Bosco exclaimed happily. "I shall never forget this nor will my boys."

"I'm glad that you are pleased", Don Cafasso smiled. "Go now to your post, and God go with you."

When Don Bosco arrived at Saint Philomena's, he found that Don Borel had made all the necessary arrangements for his boys. Madam Barola, the wealthy woman who paid for the upkeep of the home, had agreed to let his boys meet there on Sundays.

"They may use the two large rooms at the back of the building", she said. "But they must be kept away from the orphans."

When the boys arrived, Don Bosco put them to work at once. They turned one of the rooms into a chapel, the other into a game room.

Don Bosco's chief interest in his boys was to win their souls for God, but he knew that they must be kept interested and happy. Games and songs helped to make the catechism lessons more easily remembered. He still made his boys pay for his stories by listening carefully to his teaching.

The boys were very pleased with their new rooms. Bartholomew Garelli was proudest of all. Hadn't he been the one to start the club? Wasn't he its very first member?

"This place of ours ought to have a name, Father", he said.

"It certainly should", Don Bosco agreed. "I've been thinking about it."

The boys crowded around him.

"Sit down, boys," he said, "while I tell you my thoughts about a name."

As soon as they were quiet he began. "This is, above everything else, a place of prayer. Oratory is a name often given to a place of prayer. We can call it that, but we do other things here too. This is a place to study and work as well as a place to play games and sing."

He looked at Bartholomew, and the boys all began to laugh. They had often heard the story of his first meeting with the priest.

"Can you read and write", the boys teased. "No, Father, but I can sing and whistle." They imitated him perfectly. Then they all shouted with laughter.

Don Bosco and Bartholomew laughed too—the boy, with a very red face, and the priest, with a kindly pat on his shoulder.

"The whistling and the singing have proved very successful here," Don Bosco said, "especially the singing. That is one of the important things we do in our Oratory. How would it be if we called these rooms our *Festive Oratory?*"

They all agreed, and Festive Oratory became the name of their meeting place. They didn't know then that their meeting place would be the first of thousands of Don Bosco's Festive Oratories all over the world.

"We'll dedicate our Festive Oratory on the Feast of the Immaculate Conception", Don Bosco said. "We'll put all that we do here into our Lady's loving hands. But we must also have a patron saint. I have chosen one whom I believe most suitable."

"Who is he, Father?" The boys were eager to know his name.

"Saint Francis de Sales", Don Bosco replied. "He was once the bishop of Genoa."

"Tell us more about him, Father", the boys begged.

"Although he was a great bishop, he was always humble and gentle. He was loved by the poor as well as the rich. He was kind and understanding. He was patient and full of joy. People loved him for these traits and tried to be like him. This pleased him for he knew that his followers were drawing nearer to God.

"I'd like for you to be followers of Saint Francis de Sales. I'd like you to imitate his ways. Then you will be drawing nearer to God. Let's start by being patient and generous with each other and with everyone we meet."

"Even my mean old boss?" one boy called out.

Don Bosco smiled. The lesson he was teaching his boys was not an easy one to learn. "Yes, even with your mean old boss", he answered. "Who knows? He might be so surprised that he'd stop being mean."

There was a great laugh at that. All too many of the boys had mean old bosses.

"Try it, boys", Don Bosco urged. "Try it on the people you meet in your shops and on the streets. Ask our Saint Francis to help you."

The Festive Oratory numbered three hundred when a great misfortune fell upon the club. Madam Barola suddenly decided that the boys must leave the orphanage.

"They are too noisy, and they are tramping on

my flowers. Besides I need the rooms they are now using. The boys must go", she ordered.

Don Borel and Don Bosco did their best to make her change her mind. They promised that the boys would be kept quieter. They would, of course, repair any damage they had done to the gardens. In the future they would be more careful.

But no, they must leave.

"What'll we do, Father? Where can we go?" His boys could hardly believe the bad news.

"We'll find a place where we can all be together", Don Bosco assured them. "Pray to our Lady. She will take care of us, I am sure."

It was not easy to find a place for so many boys. Don Bosco tramped many miles before he found a place that might do. It was a chapel in a graveyard, a strange place for a boys' club.

Don Bosco visited the priest in charge and explained his problem.

"Of course you may use the chapel", the priest said. "We only need it weekdays for funerals. Bring your boys next Sunday."

"May they play in the meadow beyond the wall, Father?" A place to play and burn up young energy was as important as a place for teaching.

"Certainly use the meadow", said the priest. "It will be good to hear young voices in this all-too-quiet spot."

But his housekeeper did not have the same feeling. When the boys arrived the following Sunday, the priest was away. Almost as soon as they began their games and shouting, she ran out and demanded that they leave.

When the priest returned home, he could not convince her that the boys would do no harm. She had made up her mind to have her way.

"Either they go or I go", she declared.

The priest was old and ill. He needed her care and could not get along without her. He sadly agreed to tell Don Bosco not to bring his boys back.

"There must be a good reason for this", Don Bosco told his boys. "God must have another place for us. We must pray harder that he will lead us to it."

Once more the search began. Each Sunday the Happy Company met in a different place. Don Bosco called it his traveling show and made jokes about it.

"You fellows are like cabbages", he said. "They have to be transplanted several times during their growth. Each time they are taken up and planted in a new place they become stronger until they are perfect. Our Oratory will grow stronger in spite of these moves—or maybe because of them, my little cabbages."

CHAPTER EIGHT

Moving from one place to another was not Don Bosco's only hardship. His own friends tried to convince him to give up his work for his boys.

"Why do you keep on with this work?" some of them asked. "Let the boys go to their own parish churches for Mass and catechism. You are working too hard. Your health can't stand it. You will break down."

But Don Bosco shook his head. He knew his boys better than anyone else in the world. He knew that if he left them, they wouldn't go to their own parish churches or to any others. They would drift away from God and their religion.

No, he wouldn't leave them. He loved these rough, ragged boys. He knew better than anyone else that our Lord never wanted them to be that way.

Don Bosco thought again of his strange dreams of long ago. These boys were the wild beasts that had become lambs. They were his to teach and save. No, he wouldn't give them up.

Then people began to think that his mind had become affected. They'd tap their own heads and shake them in a knowing way.

"His hard work and long hours are beginning to make him a bit queer", they said. Even his best friends thought that he was saying strange things.

"He sees such a big future for his boys' club", they said. "Here he is, a priest without a penny of his own, yet he talks about churches, play-grounds, and schools as though he actually saw them."

"How can you talk about those things when you don't even have a room for the boys you've already collected?" one asked him.

"That will come", Don Bosco stated calmly. He had complete faith in his gracious Lady.

But the talkers still talked. "Why he even sees great numbers of priests, nuns, and lay people coming to help with his boys", one told another.

"Are you thinking of starting a religious order?" one asked him with a sneer.

"That's it", Don Bosco replied.

"And what kind of habit will you clothe them in?" he scoffed.

"I will clothe them in virtue", the young priest replied quietly.

"But you will need more than that, my young dreamer. Cloth for habits costs money", the man insisted.

"My order will work for it", was Don Bosco's firm reply. "Poverty and work—there is no better beginning for any order."

Then they did shake their heads. "His mind is really going", they declared. "He should be put away."

There were even some who tried to do it, but they were not successful. Don Bosco's mind was quite clear. He was not crazy, nor was he an idle dreamer. He was a man with a vision and a purpose. He knew that God and his gracious Lady would help him to make his dreams come true.

The next Sunday he sat on the stone wall that circled a meadow, teaching catechism. When the lesson ended he stood up and said, "Be off with you now. Have a good run in the field, an extra good one, for today is our last Sunday here."

"Oh, Father, we're not moving again? Your cabbages will never grow strong. They don't stay in one place long enough", one shouted. "They will wither and die."

"That will never happen", the priest replied. He smiled at them but even he was beginning to be discouraged.

His Happy Company had been forced to move five times in the past ten months. His cabbages must have a place where they could take root.

"Before you start your games, we'll visit the Church of Our Lady of the Fields and ask her to help us."

Down the road they marched, two by two. It was a long line for there were now four hundred of them. They crowded into the small village church, each with the same prayer in his heart. "Our Lady of the Fields, please find us a good meeting place."

Don Bosco added his own prayer to the Blessed Mother. "Please find us a place where we may stay."

They left the church, the boys to play in the field, Don Bosco to watch them from the stone wall.

Suddenly he noticed a man crossing the field and coming toward him.

"Father," said the stranger, "I hear that you are looking for a place for your boys."

"I am indeed", Don Bosco replied.

"I think I have just the place for you", said the man. "If you'll come with me, I'll show it to you."

Don Bosco followed him across the meadow. At the very end of it was a long, low building.

"You don't mean this place? Why this is just a

wagon shed." Desperate as he was, Don Bosco didn't see how this tumbledown shed could be of any use to him.

"I'd fix it up a bit for you, Father. It has a fairly good roof", the farmer said.

"But the roof is too low." Don Bosco was looking the place over carefully.

"Only at the back of the shed", said the farmer. "I can dig down a few feet and make the floor lower."

The priest smiled. "You mean you'll raise the roof by lowering the floor?"

"Well, something like that." He was very eager to have Don Bosco use his shed. "Your boys can play on the land around the building. I'll not charge extra for that."

"How much rent do you want?" Don Bosco asked. With some work on it, the place might hold his Happy Company.

"I'll not charge you much, Father. And you can move in before you pay."

"How about a lease?" Don Bosco didn't want to move in and move right out again. He'd had enough of that.

"You can have a year's lease, Father", said the farmer.

The thought of staying in one place for a year was enough for Don Bosco. "I'll take it", he said. "Can you have it ready for us to use next Sunday?"

"That's so soon, Father."

Don Bosco started to walk away.

The man ran after him. He didn't want to lose his new tenant. "Yes, I'll have it ready by next Sunday."

Don Bosco hurried back to tell his boys. "Your prayer is answered", he cried.

They cheered and shouted in their joy at having a meeting place of their own. But they would have been even happier if they could have looked into the future.

For someday there would be a school, workshops of all kinds, and a church—all built where Mr. Pinardi's tumbledown shed now stood.

The boys spent every possible minute the following week working on their new Oratory. Each evening after work they hurried to the shed in the field at Valdocco. They stayed as late as they could, almost falling over each other in their eagerness to help the farmer get their place ready by Sunday.

Some of the boys helped with the digging, making a great joke about raising the roof. Some cleaned and scrubbed every inch of the place. Some built their first altar.

No one took time off to rest. They wanted everything in perfect order to surprise Don Bosco when he returned from the city.

As soon as he had rented the shed, he left for Turin. He had to get the archbishop's permission to carry on his work in the new place. Also there was the little matter of money. Don Bosco had none of his own, but he had hopes of borrowing some from good friends.

Archbishop Fransoni greeted him warmly. He had ordained the young priest and had watched his work closely. When he heard Don Bosco's news he was very much pleased.

"You have my permission, my son", he said. "And you have my blessing on your work. From now on, the boys who attend your Oratory each week may look upon it as their parish church. You may hear their confessions and offer Mass there and give them Holy Communion. In fact, you may do everything for them that a pastor does, for from now on you are their pastor."

Don Bosco's heart was light as he walked swiftly toward Valdocco. At last he was truly the shepherd of a flock. His thoughts went back to his boyhood. Once again he saw the great flock of sheep his gracious Lady had placed in his charge. Once again he could hear himself say to her, "But I have no pasture. What can I do with them, my Lady?"

He could still hear her gentle answer. "Do not be afraid. I will look after you and help you."

Why had he ever doubted? She had looked after him always. He knew now that she always would. Even the first year's rent was safe in his pocket. The archbishop had pressed it into his hand when he was leaving.

"Our Lady, Help of Christians, I thank you." His prayer was almost a song as he hurried along.

The new chapel was ready on Sunday. Just eighteen months ago he and his boys had begun their meetings in the college courtyard. Now they had a real home of their own.

Small as it was, five hundred young voices rang out joyously on that Easter Sunday in 1846, "Holy, holy, holy, Lord God of hosts. Heaven and earth are filled with thy glory. Hosanna in the highest. Blessed is he who comes in the name of the Lord. Hosanna in the highest."

CHAPTER NINE

THE BOYS were now able to spend more time with Don Bosco. With a meeting place of their own, they could go there after work on weekdays as well as on Sundays.

The teaching of religion had always been of first importance wherever they met. It would still come first in the new Saint Francis de Sales Oratory. But with the extra time the young priest could teach the boys other things too.

This was the chance that Don Bosco had long

hoped for. He could now do a great deal more to help them become better men, good citizens.

Many of his young people could neither read nor write. Some never wanted to learn. Some never had the chance. Now they all wanted to join his night classes. They didn't know it then but theirs was the first night school.

As soon as the boys finished their day's work in Turin, they hurried out of the city to Valdocco. Some went without their suppers. Some ate whatever they could as they walked along. Sometimes Don Bosco gave them bread and cheese. Sometimes he added water to his own kettle of soup to make it go around among the hungry ones.

The boys enjoyed their lessons and were most eager to learn. Some learned more quickly than others. As soon as these brighter ones had learned enough, Don Bosco put them to work teaching the slower pupils. He alone couldn't possibly teach the huge classes that came each night. In order not to turn any boys away, he worked out a good plan of student teachers.

He chose his teachers not only for their high marks but also for their good conduct and common sense. He selected them carefully, for Don Bosco's standards were always high.

As the number of student teachers grew, Don Bosco offered more subjects. Besides religion, reading, and writing, the boys were taught arithmetic.

That subject was very important. Most of his boys couldn't figure well enough to know whether or not they were paid correctly. Some of them had bosses who took advantage of their lack of learning. Don Bosco wanted to put an end to that.

As soon as a number of classes in the basic subjects were being taught in his night school, Don Bosco added history, geography, and languages. Don Cafasso, Don Borel, and several other priests helped whenever they could spare time from their own work.

The school grew rapidly. Soon more space was needed for classrooms. Don Bosco was able to buy a building near the big shed. The owner was willing to sell to the priest at a very low price.

With more space for his classes, Don Bosco began to teach the trades, arts, and sciences. He wanted his boys to have whatever they needed to round out their education. He had taken care of their souls and minds. Now he must see that they became skillful with their hands.

Everything that he had learned as a boy now became useful to him. He remembered his own hardships when he worked for the tailor, the baker, and the shoemaker. His boys learned all these trades.

Don Bosco's love of music led to a fine boys' choir. The Happy Company was invited to sing in some of the city's biggest churches. People in the street stopped to watch them march in lines from the Oratory to the place where they were to sing.

"They'd make a fine band as well as a good choir", one man declared. "I have a piano I'll give to them."

The piano was sent to the Oratory. It was not a very good one, but Don Bosco was able to make it work. Each night when the boys had finished their lessons, they gathered around and sang some Italian songs. Then before they left for their long walk back to the city, they sang good-night hymns to God and his Blessed Mother.

Don Bosco's own work began at dawn. Many of his boys attended daily Mass. Some of them came to church very early so that they could go to confession before receiving Communion. No matter how early they came, he was there ahead of them and heard their confessions before he began his Mass.

After Mass he went to his rooms where he cooked and ate a hurried breakfast.

Next he visited the prisons and hospitals to comfort and help the troubled, the sick, and the dying. Then he called on the merchants and factory owners to find jobs for his young people or straighten out their problems.

He went to the homes of the rich to ask for money for his growing schools. Nothing was too much for him to do for his beloved children.

At the end of each long, tiring day he hurried

home to cook his small supper of the plainest food. Then it was time to teach his night classes.

All this work was too much for one person. Don Bosco's friends warned him that he would break down, but he had to keep on. His boys needed every minute that he could give them. There was no one else who could or would take care of them the way he did.

But finally the hard-working priest became ill. Frightened, loving friends carried him to his bed.

"It is pneumonia", the doctors said. "He has not the strength to fight it. He cannot possibly live."

Those were words of doom to the boys who waited anxiously for news of their beloved friend. Death was to take him away from them.

"It can't be", moaned one big fellow. He was not ashamed of the tears on his cheek. "Let's all pray that God will let us keep him."

He led the way to the chapel. The boys took turns before the Blessed Sacrament. Boys knelt there day and night every minute of the long illness of Don Bosco.

Don Borel came to take care of his dear friend. Other priests did their best to keep the school going, but the boys couldn't keep their minds on their lessons. They could think of only one thing. Don Bosco must not die.

"Tell him that we need him", the boys begged Don Borel.

"I have told him that over and over again", replied the priest. "He loves you all, but he says it is God's will that he be taken from you."

"We'll not let him go", the boys sobbed. "We'll be lost without him."

It was true. Many of them would be lost without Don Bosco. Others would try to carry out his work, but it would not be the same.

Don Borel again knelt beside his dying friend. "Don Bosco", he whispered. "Your work on earth is not finished."

"It must be." Don Bosco was so weak he could barely say the words. "It is God's will that I go home to him."

"If only you would ask him to make you well", Don Borel pleaded. "He would grant your prayers."

Don Bosco smiled. "To please you, my good friend, I will pray. Lord, if it is your will, cure me for the sake of my boys."

Then he closed his eyes and slept.

Don Borel rose from his knees. There was a light of joy in his eyes.

"He will recover", he whispered to the boy anxiously waiting outside the door.

"He will recover." The messenger carried the words to those in the chapel. The good news passed quickly from one to another.

"He will recover." Now they offered prayers of thanksgiving for the refreshing sleep God had sent to the sick man.

"He will recover." Their joy could not be put into words. Don Bosco would return to them.

Don Bosco did recover, but his health returned very slowly. When he was better, the doctors told him that he must go away to rest and regain his strength.

"I'll go home to Becchi", he decided. "My mother will put fat on my bones. The sun and good air will bring color to my cheeks."

Don Bosco spent three months in the Becchi hills. When at last he was able to return to Valdocco, he asked his mother to go with him.

"We need a mother at the Oratory", he said. "Would you be willing to keep house for me and help me with my boys?"

"Yes, John, I'll gladly go with you. My work here is done. It will be hard for me to leave your brother Joseph and his wife. I shall miss them and my grandsons. But now I think that I can best serve God by helping you."

They walked the ten miles to Valdocco. Don Bosco carried a small basket of food. His mother carried a bundle that held a few of her personal treasures. Her son didn't know it then but Margaret Bosco had brought her wedding dress with her. When the time came, she would sell it and use the money for altar linens for the chapel of Saint Francis de Sales Oratory.

As they neared Valdocco they met a priest. They stopped to talk to him.

"Good morning, good morning", Don Vola greeted Don Bosco. "I hear you have been ill."

"Oh, that is a thing of the past", Don Bosco replied. "Now I am well again and on my way back to work. I'd like you to meet my mother. She is going with me to help as only a mother can."

Don Vola smiled. "You have need of her. Don't let your son work too hard. That is a fault of his."

"I'll do my best, Father", she replied. "But it takes more than a mother to hold him back."

"I'm sure of that", the priest replied. "You have chosen a good housekeeper, Don Bosco. Do you have money to pay her?"

"This one works for love", Don Bosco laughed. "She will take no pay."

"Love of God and love of her son! But even those who work for love must eat." Don Vola felt around in his pockets. "I have no money", he said after a thorough search. "But, here, take my watch. Sell it and use the money toward your good work."

Don Bosco thanked him warmly. "You see, Mother," he said, as they went on their way, "the good Lord takes care of us."

When they reached the Oratory, Don Bosco led the way to his living quarters. "This is my room, Mother, with the kitchen next to it. Yours is on the other side of the kitchen."

"It is all very nice, John", she said. And she

never let him know that she was a little disappointed. "It's all very small and crowded", she thought. "Much smaller than our rooms at home. But I shall do my best to make him comfortable."

Margaret began work at once.

"Go into your room, John, and rest", she ordered as she tied on her apron. "I have things to do that only a woman can do."

Don Bosco obeyed as though he were once more her little boy. Margaret cleaned and scrubbed and sang as she worked. She was happy to turn the small, bare room into a pleasant home for her priest son.

When his boys found out that Don Bosco had returned, they came at once to welcome him. It didn't take them long to learn that his mother was to be a mother to all of them. They called her Mother Margaret, and to this day Don Bosco's boys all over the world call her Mother Margaret.

CHAPTER TEN

S OON AFTER his return from Becchi Don Bosco was as hard at work as he had been before his illness. His classes kept on growing so rapidly that he had to find more room for them. After much searching he found a suitable place for a low price near the center of the city.

"We shall name our new Oratory after Saint Aloysius", he announced the day it opened. "He is the saint of purity and a fine model for young people. When evil thoughts tempt you, he will help you to overcome them. Pray to him."

The Oratory of Saint Aloysius was soon over-crowded, and it became necessary to find a third place for classes. Don Bosco named this one the Guardian Angel Oratory.

"You each have a guardian angel", he told the new students. "God gave him to you when you were born. This angel will never leave you during life. He will take you home to God when your life ends. Your angel is your friend and protector. He tells you what is right and what is wrong. Listen carefully for he speaks softly within your heart."

Don Bosco loved his own guardian angel and the saints. They helped him in everything he tried to do. He prayed with greatest fervor to our Lord in the Blessed Sacrament. And he always asked God's Mother to beg special blessings for him from her Son.

"Our Lady, Help of Christians", he would pray. "Take care of these boys. Please help me find the rent for our new Oratory, the food for our table, the words to reach the hearts of my boys."

His gracious Lady never failed him. She saw to it that Don Bosco's boys were always taken care of.

No matter how many boys came to join his classes, Don Bosco never felt that he had too many. In fact, he kept right on looking for more. Often at night he walked through the dark city streets after his classes were over. It didn't matter to him that he was tired and should have been in bed. This was the time that the roughest boys were prowling around. They were the ones who needed him the most. This was the time to find them.

One night as he passed a dark alley he heard running footsteps. He followed them calling out, "Don't run away, boys. I haven't come to harm you. I am your friend."

One by one they came out of their hiding places.

"Why did you run away?" Don Bosco asked.

The biggest and boldest spoke up.

"You're a priest", he said. There was no sign of respect in the way he said it. "We don't like priests. If you know what's good for you, you'd better be on your way."

"I know what's good for me", Don Bosco answered. "But do you know what's good for you?"

"Indeed we do", two or three shouted. "A couple of drinks would be good for us right now. How about it, fellows?"

Everyone agreed. "Drinks for all of us", they shouted.

Don Bosco raised his hand to silence them. "Drinks for all of you", he repeated. "Very well then. Drinks it shall be. Come, follow me."

He led the way to a tavern.

"Must be some trick", the boys muttered to each other. "A priest treating us to drinks."

But their curiosity was great enough to make them follow him.

"A table for twenty", Don Bosco said to the astonished waiter.

"Yes, Father. Yes, Father." He hurried away

to pull out chairs. Most of his customers stood at the bar, and never before had he seen a priest inside the place.

"What's the world coming to?" the waiter thought.

The boys chose whatever they liked, and the waiter went off to fill their order. As soon as he was gone, Don Bosco talked pleasantly with the boys.

"You're different from other priests", the boldest one said as he drank his wine.

"Maybe you know me better", replied Don Bosco. "What parish do you belong to?"

"We don't belong to any", was the answer.

"Where do you go to Mass?" Don Bosco questioned.

"We don't go to Mass", the boy replied promptly.

Don Bosco said no more. When they had finished their drinks, he rose from the table.

"It's very late, boys. We'd better be getting home."

"Most of us don't have homes", said one.

"Where do you sleep?" Don Bosco asked.

"In doorways or in barns or wherever we can find a place", he replied. "We try a different one each night."

"Those of you who have homes, go along now", Don Bosco said. "Those who haven't homes may come with me. I'll find room in my house for you."

"All of us?" The boys couldn't believe their good fortune.

"Yes, all of you, my sons", the priest said to the astonished group. "And it would please me if you called me Father."

Mother Margaret was waiting up for her son. She sat beside the kitchen table working on her huge pile of mending.

"I've brought you some overnight guests, Mother." Don Bosco led the crowd of rough looking boys into the room.

Mother Margaret put down the sock she was darning. "Your friends are most welcome, but I must figure out a place for them to sleep."

"How about the hayloft at the top of the shed?" her son suggested.

"That would do nicely", she agreed. "You take them there while I find blankets for them."

That night the boys were more comfortable than they had been in their lives. Don Bosco left them with his blessing and returned to his own room.

He was very pleased with his night's work. It had long been his dream to have a boarding school for his boys. Maybe this was its beginning.

It didn't turn out to be a very good beginning, for in the morning when he went to call his guests to breakfast they were gone. They had left without a thank you and had taken with them Mother Margaret's blankets.

One evening a short time later while Don Bosco and his mother were eating their supper, someone knocked at the door. Don Bosco opened it to find a stranger. He was wet and cold.

"Come in, come in", the priest said. A boy of about fourteen stepped inside.

"Why are you out on such a rainy night?" Don Bosco asked. "Your clothes are wringing wet. We must find some dry ones for you. Mother Margaret, we have a guest."

There was a twinkle in his mother's eyes. "Is he like the last guests you brought home?" she asked.

Don Bosco smiled. He knew his mother was thinking of her missing blankets. "We shall see, but the boy is wet and cold and by the looks of him, quite hungry."

That was all Mother Margaret needed. She hurried away to find dry clothes. While the boy changed into them, she poured out a bowl of hot soup.

The boy ate as though he were starving.

"You've been a long time without food", Don Bosco said kindly.

"Since yesterday, sir", the boy replied. "I've come from Chieri."

"That's quite a long way. Why are you here?" the priest asked.

"I've come to the city to look for work", he answered.

"Where are your parents?"

"My father died a long time ago." The boy stopped for a moment. There were tears in his eyes. "My mother died just a week ago. The man who owned our house told me to get out. He said he'd keep the furniture to pay the rent my mother couldn't pay. Someone told me about you. I came here to see if you could find work for me."

He sat back in his chair, warmed by the food but very tired.

Mother Margaret took away the empty bowl. "I'll fix a bed for you", she said.

"Won't that be too much trouble?" the boy asked politely.

"Not at all", Mother Margaret said with a smile. Then she looked at her son. "We're quite used to overnight guests."

Later when the tired boy was warmly tucked into bed, she sat beside him.

"You are so kind", he said. "You make me think of my own mother."

"Would you like to tell me about her?" Mother Margaret asked gently.

"Oh, yes", said the boy. And he told her about his home life and the mother he missed so much.

"Your mother is in heaven now, and she will watch over you. And you know, my dear, you have God's Mother to take care of you too." Then she told him about our Lady and knelt beside him to say a Hail Mary.

"God bless you, my boy. May his angels watch over you." She blew out the candle and left him to more pleasant dreams than he'd had for a long time.

Don Bosco found work for the boy in Turin.

Each evening he came home to Mother Margaret. The overnight guest had come to stay. It was he who began Don Bosco's boarding home for boys.

He was the first boarder, but before long there were many more. They came one by one until there were thirty boys crowded into the little house and hayloft. No one seemed to mind the crowding, and Mother Margaret called them all her sons.

They were a cheerful, happy group. Some worked in the mills and the factories. Some were learning to be shoemakers. Some were learning to be carpenters. None of them earned very much, but each payday they came stamping into the house, calling, "Mother Margaret. Where is Mother Margaret? We have something for you."

She'd leave her stove where she was cooking their supper and hold out her apron. They would all laugh merrily as they marched by, dropping the money they had earned into her apron.

"Ah, that coin will buy a soup bone for us", she said. "And this one will buy the flour for our bread. This one will take care of the vegetables we need. Now my apron is full and our cupboard will be too. Oh, no, here is one more coin. That will give us a nice pie for Sunday. We are rich this week."

And indeed they were rich, not in money but in the warm love of a happy home. They were rich in the friendship and help of Don Bosco. They were rich in the loving prayers of Mother Margaret.

Each night she talked to her boys and sometimes told them the same stories she had told to her own sons long ago. The orphan boy who had come from Chieri had been the first boarder to enjoy her nightly talks. These talks have become a custom in all the Salesian homes all over the world. Today they are still given by one of the priests or brothers.

CHAPTER ELEVEN

Aᴌᴌ ᴅᴜʀɪɴɢ his teaching years Don Bosco tried to make saints out of his boys. In 1954, one of his first boarders, Dominic Savio, was named a saint. He was born in the same part of Italy as his teacher but about twenty-seven years later.

When Dominic was just a little boy his parents taught him a great deal about his religion. He learned easily, and when he was only five their pastor taught him to serve Mass.

There were those who said, "He is too young."

"Age doesn't matter", the priest told them. "He

serves better than some much older and not as pure in heart."

When he was seven Dominic begged to be allowed to make his First Holy Communion. His mother had taught him his catechism well, and when the pastor questioned him he knew every answer perfectly.

"You may receive with the older children", the priest said joyfully. He believed that Dominic was especially loved by our Lord.

Dominic always spoke of the day of his First Communion as the best day of his life. On that day, although he was only seven, he wrote four promises in a notebook. They were his rules for the way he promised to live, and he never broke that promise.

1. I will go to confession often, and to Communion as often as my confessor will allow.
2. I will keep holy the feast days.
3. My friends will be Jesus and Mary.
4. Death but not sin.

By the time he was ten Dominic had received all the schooling he could get in his own village. He was a good student and he wanted more schooling, but his parents couldn't pay for any more tuition.

"Can't I go to the free school in Castlenuova?" he begged.

"It is too far", his father answered. "The ten-mile walk each day would be too much for you."

Dominic was not very strong, but he had a great desire to learn. "The walk won't hurt me", he insisted. "Please let me go."

"We can let him try", his mother suggested. And his father agreed.

So Dominic began his long daily walks to and from school. One day as he trudged along the hot, dusty road, a stranger stopped him.

"I've often seen you on this road", said the stranger. "Where do you go, my boy?"

"I go to school in Castlenuova", Dominic answered.

"This road is dangerous. Aren't you afraid to travel by yourself?" asked the man.

"I'm not alone", the boy replied.

The man looked around.

Dominic smiled. "You can't see my friend", he said. "But he is with me just the same."

"Who is he?" the man asked.

"My guardian angel", replied Dominic. "He is with me wherever I go."

"Don't you ever get tired?" the man asked.

"I don't think about being tired", Dominic answered. "I work for a good Master. He gives me good pay."

"Most people complain about the ones they work for. Who is the good master who pays you so well?"

"Our Lord", Dominic replied. "I work for him as well as I can. Good day, sir."

"God and his angel!" the man walked off muttering to himself. "It's a long time since I've thought of such things. Maybe I'll try to make friends with them again."

Dominic Savio did unusually well at school. He was soon at the head of his class. He entered into all the school games and fun and was liked by the boys and the teachers.

One spring morning on the way to school, some of his friends stopped by a little stream. "Come along, Dominic, we're all going swimming", they said. "Let's not go to school today."

The water looked tempting but Dominic shook his head.

"Tomorrow you can say you stayed home because you were sick", they suggested to him.

By this time they had reached the river. Some of the boys were already in the water. Some were standing around telling jokes that never should have been told.

"I'm going to school", Dominic declared. "There are at least two sins connected with this fun. A lie and impurity. No, thank you." And off he went.

Dominic was thinking about his First Communion promises. "Death but not sin."

"Probably those fellows don't know that some things that seem like fun are really sins", he thought. "When I grow up I'm going to be a priest and teach young people what is right and what is wrong."

A short time later Dominic had a most unhappy experience at school. He was accused of doing something extremely wrong.

"If it were any other boy but you, Dominic," the teacher scolded, "I might be able to understand. But an honor student, respected by teachers and pupils!"

The teacher paused. He seemed sad rather than angry.

"You do not deny your guilt so you must take your punishment. Come here where all the class can see you."

Dominic walked slowly to the front of the room.

"Face your friends", the teacher ordered. "Let them see the boy they all admired. Let them see the punishment you have brought on yourself.

"You should be thrown out of school", the teacher went on. "Any other boy would have been sent home at once. Because this is your first offense, you may have another chance. I shall not even give you the beating you deserve, but I hope your shame is punishment enough. Go back to your place."

At recess the boys whispered to each other about Dominic, but no one went near him. The next day as soon as school began the teacher shouted angrily, "Dominic Savio, come here!"

Poor Dominic again walked slowly to the front of the room and faced the class.

"Young man, I have an apology to make", the teacher began. "Yesterday I accused you of doing something very wrong. Since then I have found out who was really guilty. He will be thrown out of school. Why did you keep still when you were falsely accused?"

"Sir, I didn't want the guilty one sent home", said Dominic. "He had been in trouble before. It was my first time. I thought I would be given another chance."

"But wasn't it hard to be accused of something you had not done?" asked the teacher.

"Yes, sir. But I tried to be like Someone else who was falsely accused. He didn't complain."

When Dominic had completed the course at the free school his teachers wanted him to have more schooling.

"How would you like to go to Don Bosco's school in Turin?" Don Cugliero asked him.

"I would, Father, more than I can say", Dominic replied eagerly. "But my parents can't afford to give me any more schooling."

Later Don Bosco visited the free school, and Dominic was sent to talk to him.

"I hear you would like to come to our school", Don Bosco said.

"Oh, yes, Father. More than anything else in the world!"

"Tell me why, my son", said Don Bosco.

"I'd like to study Latin and become a priest",

Dominic replied. "There is another reason. I have never told this one to anyone else. Father, I want to become a saint."

Don Bosco looked deep into the boy's eyes. "Yes," he said, "I believe you have the material to become a priest and a saint."

"If I have the material will you be the tailor?" Dominic asked earnestly.

"I will indeed, my son. Together we'll turn out a fine garment for our Lord."

Dominic entered the Oratory of Saint Francis de Sales in October 1854. He studied hard and learned quickly. He was a friendly boy and was very much troubled when any of his schoolmates argued or fought. He always did his best to keep peace.

One day he saw two young boys fighting on the playground. He tried to break up the battle but they turned on him.

"Just stay out of this, will you?" they shouted.

The boys were extremely angry. It was the worst fight Dominic had ever seen. They were even hitting each other with rocks. Finally the boys grew tired, but their anger had not cooled. While they rested Dominic stepped between them.

"We're not stopping, Dominic", they both declared.

"I'm not asking you to", replied Dominic. "I could report you and have a teacher stop the fight, but I won't. All I ask is that you each go to the opposite sides of the field and begin again. Wait for my signal."

They agreed, but each boy took with him some good-sized rocks. Dominic took his place in the center of the field.

"Now throw!" he shouted.

"We can't throw rocks at you, Dominic. You aren't going to trick us that way. Step aside or you'll get hurt." They were angrier than ever.

"If you won't throw stones at me," Dominic called out, "throw them at him." He took a small crucifix out of his pocket and held it up high. "Your rocks can't hurt him any more than your anger does."

There was a complete silence. Then suddenly the boys were ashamed. They remembered that that kind of anger is a sin.

Dominic saw that they were ready to stop. "Come, let's shake hands all round and forget the whole thing."

And they did.

Dominic's life was full of courage in the simple, everyday things. He had temptations like other boys, but he overcame them in the right way. He never forgot his First Communion promises. Death rather than sin was firmly fixed in his mind and heart.

When he had been at school only three years he became very ill. He was only fifteen. He wanted so much to finish his schooling and become a priest, but that was not meant to be. The doctors decided that he must be sent home. He took his disappointment bravely and accepted it as God's will.

"You'll come back, my son", Don Bosco said as Dominic left the Oratory.

"No, Father. I shall not come back", he replied quietly. "Please pray for me."

Don Bosco laid his hand on the boy's head and blessed him.

"Good-bye, Dominic", he said gently. "I'll pray to you, not for you."

Not long afterward, news came that Dominic Savio had gone home to God. He died on March 9, 1857. A few weeks later his father awoke one night to see someone standing beside him.

"It is I, Father, your Dominic. Do not be frightened. I have come to tell you that I am in heaven."

Then he was gone.

His father knew that it was not a dream. His son had truly appeared to him.

Dominic's schoolmates believed he was a saint while he was living. After his death they began to pray to him and their prayers were answered. God granted many miracles through Dominic Savio.

The years passed, and the proofs necessary for his canonization were given to the Church. On June 12, 1954, Pope Pius XII pronounced the young schoolboy a saint.

Today young people all over the world claim

him for their very own. Some call him the teenage saint. Some call him the classroom saint, but all boys and girls can call him the children's saint for Dominic Savio truly belongs to them. They try to be like him and keep the simple rules by which he lived.

CHAPTER TWELVE

A S HIS CLASSES GREW it became harder for Don Bosco to get books for his students. He couldn't possibly buy enough books, and many of the ones that he had were dull and uninteresting. Some of them, especially the histories, were not even truthful.

"If I can't buy the right books for my boys, I'll make them", he decided.

First of all he prayed.

"Our Lady, Help of Christians, your boys need books. Please show me how to get them."

Soon after that, one of his night school students came to him and said, "Father, my boss is getting a new printing press. He said that you could have the old one without paying him any money if you would take it away quickly. He needs the space."

At once a dozen boys offered to go after it. They returned with the old printing press and a box of well-worn type.

"Now if we only had paper we could start printing our books", Don Bosco said.

One of the boys spoke up. "Father, I work for a man who makes paper. Maybe he will give us some."

The man proved to be most generous. He sent Don Bosco a good supply to start with and more as it was needed. In no time at all some of the classrooms were humming with the pleasant sound of a print shop.

As fast as Don Bosco wrote, his boys were taught to print and bind. These skills soon became a part of the Oratory program.

The first book to come from the Oratory Press was a Bible history. Don Bosco wrote the stories as simply as he told them. Next he wrote a history of Italy. That too was interesting and truthful.

At that time, just as today, a few evil people were trying to do away with religion. They printed booklets and papers and handed them out on the streets and in the factories. The writings were planned to destroy belief in God.

Some of the young people who read them were foolish enough to believe the printed lies. They began to scoff at the Faith. They joined the group that was doing this evil work and drifted away from the sacraments.

Their new leaders taught them to hate the Church and her priests. They taught them that all holy works were a waste of time. Even some of the Oratory boys were drawn into this trap.

Don Bosco talked earnestly to all of his boys about the harm that was being done.

"You are the ones who can save these poor souls", he said. "Talk to them, my sons. Explain the truths of our religion to the boys with whom you work. Talk to the ones who stop you in the streets."

"But, Father, they won't listen to us", the boys replied. "They call us old-fashioned and stupid. They tell us not to listen to you or any priest."

The hot temper of John Bosco, the boy, flashed into the eyes of Don Bosco, the priest. Those evil ones would not send his boys to hell! Not while he could work against them.

The presses in his print shop began to hum without stopping. The boys took turns day and night to keep them running at all hours. The lamp in Don Bosco's room seemed never to go out. He used every moment that he could spare from all his other work for writing.

As fast as he wrote his boys printed and bound.

Schoolbooks came first. His most important job was to teach his own students. Once they were filled with the truth they would carry it to others.

Then he began to print booklets. His boys handed out his good booklets at the same places where the evil ones were being given away.

Next he wrote and printed a magazine called *The Friend of Youth*. This was given out free not only to his own boys but also to anyone who wanted a copy. All of these writings were an answer to those who would destroy belief in God.

Catholic Readings was the next magazine he brought out. It was planned for family reading. In it were stories of the saints, Bible stories, and simple explanations of religion. This too was given out without any charge.

The people enjoyed all of these writings. They were interesting to the parents as well as the children. Don Bosco's boys began to give them out in front of the churches at novenas, missions, and retreats. He worked hard to supply the growing demand for them.

The enemy fought back. They printed more booklets and told more lies than they had before Don Bosco began opposing them. But they could not win against God and truth.

Soon the people turned back to Don Bosco. Everyone praised him for the good he was doing. But he would not take any credit for himself.

"It is our young people", he declared. "If they

are taught the right way of life by word and example, they will walk in the right path. If they know what is true and good, they will not turn to what is false and evil. We must teach them to work for the glory of God and the good of his children. It is our young people who will win the battle. The praise belongs to them."

CHAPTER THIRTEEN

B UT THE BATTLE between Don Bosco and the evil ones was not over. They had not been able to spread their false teaching as rapidly and thoroughly as they had hoped. All the priests stood in their way, especially Don Bosco. He must be done away with as soon as possible. That should not be too difficult.

Don Bosco often walked the city streets late at night in search of homeless boys. He always went alone. The job could be done quietly, and no one would know who committed the murder.

Mother Margaret worried a great deal about these night walks. "You should not go alone through the dark alleys. Why not take some of your boys with you?" she asked.

"Now Mother, don't worry about me", Don Bosco replied. "The boys need their sleep, and I need your prayers. Your Rosary will keep me safe."

"Of course you have my prayers always", his mother sighed. "But your boys are young and strong. They would not miss their sleep. They'd be there to stand between you and danger."

Don Bosco never thought of danger to himself. He knew that there were robbers and murderers lurking in the alleys of Turin. He had talked to some. He had rescued several of their young pupils and taught them a decent way to earn their living. He had no fear for his own safety.

One night as he left Turin and began his long walk back to Valdocco, he felt that he was being followed. As he walked along the quiet streets, he heard footsteps behind him. Then when he reached the outskirts of the town, the footsteps seemed to be beside him on the other side of the hedge. As he passed a grove of trees, he was sure that someone was hiding there and watching him.

He kept right on walking. Now he no longer heard the quiet footsteps. His follower must have passed him, hidden from his sight by the trees.

Suddenly he saw a man rushing toward him. Before Don Bosco could step aside or even call out, a cloak was thrown over his head. He struggled to free himself, but he was thrown to the ground.

"Gag him while I tie him up", he heard one man whisper.

"Why bother? No one could hear him even if he did call out", a second voice said.

"We're not taking any chances", the first one insisted. "He's had this coming to him for a long time. Here, help me lift him into the woods."

There was a low, angry growl. Before the men could move John Bosco, a huge dog leaped at them. They lay sprawling in the road, terrified.

"Call off your dog! Call off your dog, Don Bosco! He'll tear us apart. Save us, save us", they screamed.

At once the dog stopped growling. He walked over to the priest who was lying on the ground.

"Take this cloak off my head", Don Bosco demanded.

The dog stood still for a few seconds. Then he walked a few steps away.

Fearfully the two men got up from the ground. They quickly took the cloak from around Don Bosco. He stood up rather shakily. Then once more the dog jumped at the two men. Once more they sprawled in the dirt.

"Call off your dog, we beg you", they cried out in terror.

Don Bosco stood over them. "Have I your word that you will do no more harm?" he demanded.

"You have, you have, Father", they cried. "Let

us go. We promise we'll never trouble you again."

"Get up and be off with you," the priest said sternly, "unless you want to stay long enough to confess your sins."

But the would-be murderers were far down the road. They were eager to go their way and willing to let Don Bosco go his.

The big dog stood watching while Don Bosco brushed the dirt from his clothes. Then he started down the road toward home.

"Come along, my friend", he said. "You deserve a good supper for the way you took care of me. With all my heart, I thank you."

The dog looked up at him as though he understood every word. When they reached home Don Bosco opened the door.

"Come in, fellow", he said. "I want my mother to meet the one who saved my life."

But the big gray dog was gone.

The next day Don Bosco asked his boys if any of them had seen the dog.

But no one had seen him. "It must be one of Father's little jokes", the boys said to each other. They laughed. "You say he's a big, strong dog, Father. We couldn't have missed seeing him if he'd been around here."

Don Bosco was puzzled too. No one had seen his big gray dog. No one did see him. But every time that Don Bosco went on a dangerous mission, there was the dog waiting to go with him. He would stay close to Don Bosco until the priest was safely back home. Then he would disappear.

Don Bosco named his faithful protector Grigio, which is the Italian word for gray. Grigio served the priest for many years. No one tried to harm him while the dog was at his side.

The time came when Don Bosco no longer needed protection. Even his enemies had to admire and respect the priest who did so much not only for the young but also the old, the sick, and the poor. It was quite safe for him to go on his errands of mercy. Grigio no longer went with him.

For many years Don Bosco did not see the big gray dog. Then one night while he and a few friends were having supper in his rooms, Grigio suddenly appeared.

He came through the door, trotted over to Don Bosco's chair, and looked up into his eyes.

"Grigio, Grigio", Don Bosco greeted him joyfully. "Where have you been all these years? Are you hungry?" Don Bosco set his own plate of food down on the floor.

But Grigio did not eat.

"Are you thirsty, my friend?" He poured water into a bowl and set it down on the floor.

But Grigio did not drink.

He just kept his eyes on his master's face as though he would have spoken if he could.

Don Bosco looked into the dog's beautiful eyes and understood.

"You have come to say good-bye." There were tears in his eyes. He laid his hand gently on Grigio's head. "God bless you, my friend. I am so very grateful for all that you did for me."

Grigio stood there quietly for a moment longer, looking up into his master's eyes. Then he turned, walked through the open door, and was gone.

No one ever saw Don Bosco's dog again.

CHAPTER FOURTEEN

For a long time Don Bosco managed to carry on his work with gifts from his friends and from wealthy families. The time came when important people in the government learned the value of his work. At first they had been against his schools. It took a long time before they would admit that he could turn boys from the street into good citizens.

Then the government workers began sending problem children to him. They paid him for helping these children. This money made things a bit easier for Don Bosco. He was then able to add more rooms and buildings to his school and to feed and clothe and educate more poor boys.

The greater number of pupils meant more work for Mother Margaret, but she didn't mind. She was just as happy as her son with the arrival of each new student.

As always she was willing and eager to do everything that she could for Don Bosco's boys, but she was no longer young. She became very ill.

Her son's loving care and the prayers of his boys made her suffering easier. But the time had come for her to go home to God. Her death brought deep sorrow to all of the oratories. She had been a mother to hundreds of boys. They would all miss her, especially her own son.

As he offered Mass for her, he prayed, "Mother of God, help us now more than ever before. We no longer have our mother here on earth. Mary, Help of Christians, be our heavenly Mother in a special way."

His gracious Lady heard his prayer and answered it. From then on Don Bosco's work was unusually blessed. Some hardships kept on coming all his life, but his joys and rewards increased.

He became known all over Italy and was invited to preach in some of the largest churches. His excellent sermons were in demand for missions, novenas, and many other important services.

Don Bosco gladly accepted as many invitations

as he could. It meant that he could interest more people in his youth work. He needed more helpers now, and he hoped that others would carry on his work when he was gone. He wanted teachers for his own country. He wanted missionaries to carry his teaching across the seas.

His own schools were becoming more and more successful. His student teachers were working out very well. As soon as these young men were ready Don Bosco would send them to colleges for more advanced learning.

All of the arts, sciences, and trades were being taught in his oratories. To these he now added courses in farming and animal husbandry so that his students could learn the best way to grow crops and to care for farm animals.

Only one thing troubled him. "What will become of all these fine beginnings when my work on earth is done? There must be young priests to follow in the ways of this old one."

Several of his teachers seemed ready and willing to give their lives to God, but Don Bosco had to be sure. At the beginning of the novena before the Feast of Saint Francis de Sales, he spoke about vocations. At the end of his sermon he said, "If any of you think you have a vocation, pray about it. Ask God, his Blessed Mother, and your patron saint to direct you. Do not talk about it among yourselves. Each one must decide for himself. When the novena is over, let me know your decision."

Michael Rua was the first of Don Bosco's student teachers to offer himself to God. Three others joined him.

"We wish to spend our lives as priests. We especially want to teach the young in the way you do, Father."

Don Bosco was very happy. "Now you are truly my sons. You will make good priests and teachers. This is the beginning. The time will come when there will be thousands of you working for the same holy purpose. I shall give the Order you are starting a name to be proud of. You will be called Salesians."

"I am glad you chose that name, Father." It was Michael Rua who spoke. "Saint Francis de Sales has been our model ever since we were little boys. I can remember when I first came to the Oratory I wanted to take up the sword. I wanted to fight for the cause of Catholic truth. Then you explained how much more we could help the cause by our words and writings.

"At first I did not understand how that could be. I was young and eager. I thought the only way to fight was with one's fists."

All of the new Salesians laughed. It had been the same with them.

"I once thought that way too", Don Bosco admitted. "I had to learn that there were better ways of winning souls. It was our Lady who taught me that kindness can change the wildest ones into gentle lambs."

It took a long time to train the young Salesians to become priests. Don Bosco's standards were very high. His men had to be well educated in every subject they would need for their work. They must learn to be patient and gentle. They must be cheerful at all times. They must become as much like Saint Francis de Sales as possible. Only then would they be able to bring many souls to God.

When Don Bosco told his first small band of Salesians that they were only the beginning, he spoke truly. Today there are over eighteen thousand Salesians all over the world. His schools, which began with a dirty little boy who couldn't serve Mass, now number seven hundred or more. They are to be found in almost every country in the world.

Right here in our own United States of America there are Salesian schools in the cities of New York, Boston, Los Angeles, New Orleans, and San Francisco and in most of the dioceses of our country. There are Salesian missions in China, India, Japan, Australia, Africa, Siam, Turkey, Iran, and Egypt as well as schools in England and Ireland.

CHAPTER FIFTEEN

"Don Bosco, can't you do something for the girls of Turin?" the people asked. "They need schools too. They need the kind of help you give the boys."

Parents, priests, and even bishops kept asking him that question. Finally Don Bosco felt that he was ready to do something about it.

If he did start a school for girls, he would need a good, understanding person at the head of it. He had in mind a young woman by the name of Mary Mazzarello. He knew that she was deeply religious and sensible. He had met her several years ago when she was working in a tailor's shop. At night she taught catechism to some of the other girls who worked there.

The priest praised her for her good work. After that first meeting, he had helped her with his advice. Now he decided to talk to her about starting a school for girls.

"I've come to see you, Mary, about some special work", he said. "Please tell me again how you began your good work for girls."

"He must have a good reason for asking me to repeat what he already knows", Mary thought as she began to retell her story.

"When I was a little girl, Father, I worked in the vineyards. I did this for many years, but it was too hard for me. I didn't have the strength for it. I became ill, very ill. When I was well again, I couldn't go back to such heavy work. One evening at church after the people had said the Rosary, our priest read to us from a wonderful book. It was called *The Introduction to the Devout Life*."

Don Bosco smiled. How well he knew and loved that book written by his own Saint Francis de Sales! "Yes, yes, my child, go on", he said.

"As the priest read to us, he explained the meaning of what he read. It was about living a holy life. I had never known about such things until that night. As he read I felt a great desire to live the life he described. I wanted to do something for God.

"I felt this desire so strongly that as I walked

home from church with my dearest friend Petronilla, I told her about it. She felt the same way. We began at once to make plans.

"We decided that we'd work for the village tailor. There are many girls who do that work when they are very young. They work along with much older girls before they know right from wrong. They hear evil talk and see things that they should not see. Many have never been taught a thing about religion.

"Petronilla and I decided that if we worked for the tailor we might be able to teach and help these little ones. As we sewed we offered each stitch as a prayer. We loved God very much. We believed that if we loved him enough, he would let the younger girls love us. Then we could invite them to our room in the evenings and teach them about our Lord and his Blessed Mother."

Don Bosco smiled at her. He knew how well the plan had worked. As time went on other young women joined Mary and Petronilla. Now there were twenty-six of them teaching religion and helping young girls in every way they could.

"You must know, Mary," Don Bosco said when she had finished her story, "that I have come to you for a special reason. I would like you and your group to help the Salesian priests. We want you to do the same work for girls that we now do for boys. We need women teachers for that purpose.

"You and the young women who work with

you could be the beginning of a community of sisters. You are all devoting your lives to God now. If you were bound together by holy vows, your efforts would surely be more fruitful. Think about it, my child. Talk it over with your helpers. Pray that our Lady and her Son will show you what to do. I will come for your answer one month from today."

The day Don Bosco returned was the Feast of Saint Francis de Sales. That day Mary Mazzarello was chosen by the group as the first superior of their new order.

Some months later they received their habits and were clothed on the Feast of our Lady of the Snows. Fourteen were nuns. Seven were novices. That was a happy day for them and their director, Don Bosco.

"Now I shall give you the name that is dearest to my heart", he said. "From now on you shall be called, 'Daughters of Mary, Help of Christians'. Our Lady under that beautiful name has brought me many of the blessings I have needed for my oratories. She has watched over my boys. She has blessed our schools. She has strengthened our priests and taught many of them to be saintly men.

"You will do well to take her for your model. Turn to her in every need. She was our Lord's first teacher. She knows the perfect way of teaching. She will be your greatest help and comfort in your work for her Son and his children.

"You are just a small group now, but the day

will come when you will be numbered in the hundreds. Now you will teach the girls in Turin, but some day you will be called to other great cities. Remain faithful to God and your holy vows. He will reward you."

The Daughters of Mary, Help of Christians, have now grown to over thirteen thousand. They have schools all over the world. They now teach in colleges that are run by the government as well as in their own schools.

A tiny seed planted long ago in the village of Mornese, Italy, has grown into a great tree with branches in Europe, Asia, and America. The work of Mary Mazzarello and her helpers was blessed even beyond the dreams of Don Bosco. The young woman whose greatest desire was to work for God received his greatest reward. Mary Mazzarello died May 14, 1888. Not long after, the Church named her as one of God's chosen saints.

Don Bosco had now made certain that his young people would always be taught and taken care of as he planned. He had established orders of priests, brothers, and nuns to carry on his work.

One more group of Don Bosco's helpers needed to be permanently established. That group was made up of workers who did not belong to a religious order but who helped the priests and nuns in every way that they could.

These helpers began their work under Mother Margaret's direction. When the Salesian family of boys grew too large for her to do all their mending and darning, other women helped her. They joined her in making beautiful linens for the altars as well as bandages for the hospitals. These women did everything they could to assist Mother Margaret in her work for Don Bosco and his boys.

Their husbands, sons, and brothers helped too. They raised money for new schools and churches, and they found jobs for Don Bosco's boys. They coached them and built scenery for their plays. They took children to and from distant churches. They all worked willingly and happily. Many of them found this service a good way to thank God for their own blessings.

Don Bosco's first group of Salesian Co-operators was just a small band of willing workers. Today there are many of these helpers in all parts of the world.

The Salesian groups have kept on growing through the years. Their schools now prepare young people for places in all the professions, sciences, arts, and trades. A great work grew from a very small beginning.

CHAPTER SIXTEEN

Almost fifty years of Don Bosco's life had gone by. All those years he had worked night and day for young people. He was the first to find a cure for juvenile delinquency. He was the first to find a good way to prevent it. He was the first to turn large groups of wayward boys and girls into good and useful citizens in the eyes of God and man.

It never mattered to him if he only had a few hours sleep at night. It never mattered to him that his food was poor and that there was very little of it. It never mattered to him how many hours he spent in the confessional. He made sure that he gave spiritual help to anyone who wanted it. It never mattered to him how many miles he walked to beg for his boys. Nothing mattered except to bring them to God and God to them.

The time came at last when his tired legs could no longer carry him. His kindly eyes could no longer see.

His friends called one doctor, then another and another. The learned doctors shook their heads. "He cannot live much longer", they all agreed.

"Has he some sickness that cannot be cured?" his worried friends asked.

"No, there is no special illness", the doctors replied. "It is just that he is worn out. He is like a lamp that flickers and burns low. It will soon go out, for the oil is gone."

"Is there anything that we can do for him?" asked his friends.

"There is only one thing that can help him", the doctors said. "He must have rest."

But Don Bosco would not rest. "I have all eternity for that", he said cheerfully.

He would not stay in bed. "There are still important things for me to do", he declared. Then he would call one or another of his boys to help him.

Wherever he went Don Bosco now needed someone to lean upon. He who had spent his whole life in leading others now had to be led by his own boys.

As soon as he appeared on the streets, crowds

gathered around him. They wanted to touch the clothes that he wore. They wanted his blessing. They called him "our saint" while he was still on earth.

Don Bosco had always lived so close to our Lord that God gave him power to perform some of his miracles. Don Bosco had cured the sick and made the lame walk. He had given sight to the blind, and at least on one strange occasion had brought the dead back to life. God had let him perform miracles that only saints can perform.

But Don Bosco was not born a saint. Through God's grace and his own heroic effort he became one. From the time he was a young boy he did the usual, everyday things of life unusually well. He never turned away from his strong purpose.

Even sitting up at last became too great a strain on Don Bosco. He could no longer leave his bed. Again the doctors were called.

"The light is burning low", they said. Then the sorrowful words, "It has gone out." That was on January 31, 1888.

But Don Bosco's lamp has never gone out. It burns brighter with each passing year. It burns brighter with each new pupil who brings honor to his schools. It burns brighter with each newly ordained Salesian. It burns brighter with each young woman who becomes one of his Daughters of Mary, Help of Christians. Don Bosco's lamp will never go out.

He no longer belongs only to the country in which he was born. He belongs to the whole world.

For on Easter Sunday in the year 1934, eighty thousand people gathered in Saint Peter's Square in Rome to hear him named a saint. Pope Pius XI read the words of canonization:

"I do pronounce him saint, worthy to receive public honor. I do command that he receive the veneration due to a chosen one of God. I proclaim the day of his death, January thirty-first, to be his feast day, a time of rejoicing, for that day marks his entrance into heaven.

"He shall have his own Mass. Prayers shall be composed to him. His relics are to be venerated in the churches. Altars are to be dedicated to him.

"Pray to him especially those who teach the young, and the young who would learn the truth. He did much for you while he lived on earth. He can do far more for you now that he is in heaven.

"The shepherd boy of Becchi, the acrobat who juggled to win souls for God, the priest and teacher of boys, the builder of schools and churches, the founder of missions, known as Don Bosco, beloved Apostle of Youth, is now and forever, Saint John Bosco, Giant of Sanctity."